CAPTAIN JACK
GOES TO
NORTH
ALASKA

CAPTAIN JACK GOES TO NORTH ALASKA

JOHN BRICKWEDEL

ARPress
45 Dan Road Suite 5
Canton MA 02021

Hotline: 1(888) 821-0229
Fax: 1(508) 545-7580

Ordering Information:
Quantity sales. Special discounts are available on quantity purchases by corporations, associations, and others. For details, contact the publisher at the address above.

Printed in the United States of America.

ISBN-13:   Paperback   979-8-89356-664-2
                           eBook   979-8-89356-665-9

Library of Congress Control Number: 2024903629

Edited by Beverly White

Author, Educator, Great Sister.

CONTENTS

THE AUTHOR

This story is just a story and will probably never happen. When you get old you still have dreams but not a lot of time left to make them happen. I have gone to the Islands to do some research for the book so the descriptions and names of the places are as good as I can make them. If you go up to the Islands of southeast Alaska you won't find the people of the story. They are all Products of my imagination. I hope you enjoy reading the story as much as I enjoyed writing it.

CHAPTER 1

We had been to Alaska twice on the cruise ships. They hit Ketchikan and Juneau and Skagway. But I wanted to see all the other towns in the lower Islands, so I took the ferry up out of Bellingham. It stopped at more places, and I liked the boat ride. Without the cruise director telling me when to eat and what to look at and that there is gambling in the casino.

The ferry takes cars, and campers and some trucks and a lot of people. I paid for a cabin, so I didn't have to sleep on the deck. Some people did. The cabin was small but since I was traveling alone it was good enough for me.

They left the dock in the afternoon, and I was a little disappointed that I wouldn't get to see a lot of the Islands before dark. But it was August and stays light late so by dark I was ready for some sleep. Besides, in the next few days I was going to see a lot of forest and Island and clear water scenery. You can't believe how clear the water is. You can count the starfish on the bottom at three fathoms. (18 ft.) Well almost.

About dinner time I thought that I had better check out the restaurant and went looking. When I found it so had a lot of others, the line was only about halfway around the ship. (About 16 people) But I got in line anyway. I wanted something to eat before breakfast. I had soup and salad. I figured it would be quick and not hold up the people behind me. The salad was fresh, and the soup was good clam chowder. I was soon back out on deck to watch the San Juan Islands go by. You see some houses on these Islands. And as we sailed by a small harbor there were a lot of boats and the buildings of a small town. It was beautiful. I thought to myself, self, I wouldn't mind living here when I retire.

Oh, yea I'm already retired. Well almost, I'm seventy-two, but don't feel it. If it wasn't for the grey in the hair and goat beard and mustache, I'd look fifty. Or maybe forty-five.

I might as well introduce myself, I'm Jack Valines. The girls call me handsome Jack. But don't any of you guys try it. I'm an ex-marine, been in construction forever, and am half Irish and love to fight.

It was starting to get dark out on the deck and was turning a bit chilly, so I thought about going in and reading for a while before going to bed.

I was walking toward the door when looking off to the west a couple of hundred yards out there was a pod of killer whales doing their dance. So many people came out to watch that the ship started leaning to port. I watched for a few minutes and then went in.

My cabin was on the starboard side, and I weigh two hundred and fifty pounds so it might help to put the ship on an even keel again.

Daylight found me at the rail again watching the Islands slipping by. The beauty of the forest growing right down to the rocky beaches and the clear water and a boat going the other way once in a while would keep me watching most of the trip even though I had been up here before. I never got tired of it.

Where a little creek came down to the sea a pair of deer were drinking. The buck was standing guard while the doe drank, but we were too far away to worry them. I saw a lot of Eagles in the trees. A female eagle was eating something along the shore and had about a dozen crows standing around watching. Probably hoping she would leave something for them.

I was getting hungry, so I looked at my phone and it said it was time for breakfast, so I headed toward the restaurant. The deck was a little slippery from the morning dew and as I got to the door a man on crutches who was missing a leg came out. His crutch slipped on the wet deck, and he almost fell. I grabbed his arm until he was steady and said, "it's a little wet out here right now, it will dry out a little later. If you would join me for breakfast, it should be fine by the time we finish." He looked at me like he was going to refuse, and I said, "It's not much fun eating alone, and my wife didn't come with me this time. So, what do you say it's my treat?" The girl with him looked at me and said, "why not?" So, we went in and found a table and sat down.

We started by introducing ourselves then ordered. They were Dan and Carol Petrovitch. You already know my name. Handsome Jack.

Carol went through the line with me to get the food. She said, "Dan's a little grumpy since he lost his leg, don't pay any attention to it." I said, "I'd be grumpy too." They talked while they ate. Jack told them that he was thinking of moving up to Alaska and he was looking around to maybe find a place to settle. Dan said, "we moved up here when I got out of the army. We are returning from a trip to the V.A. hospital in Seattle. They are talking about giving me a peg leg." Carol said, "they want to wait until the pain of the amputation is less. But he is impatient." Jack said, "The V.A. replaced both of my hips and it took a few months before the pain was clear gone."

"Where do you live, Dan?"

"Wrangell. We found a little house there that we can afford on my disability and with what Carol makes as a waitress we make it. After I get a peg leg, I will be able to get some kind of job, and we'll be fine. Then Carol can quit and have the baby."

"Well, congratulations I hope everything works out for you."

After eating they went out on deck to watch the scenery and to get to know each other better. Jack being an ex-marine liked the Army veteran and his grit.

They got off when the ferry stopped at Bella Coola and looked around. They only had bout twenty minutes while the cars were unloaded and loaded, so they didn't get to see a whole lot. But it was a change and they enjoyed it.

The boat stopped at many little towns on the way up, but most of them you could see the whole town from the deck of the boat, and they didn't stop for long. Jack had been to Ketchikan a couple of times before, so he didn't get off there even though he had planned to. Dan and Carol invited him to stay with them in Wrangell, so he decided to take them up on it and spend a couple of days there.

When they got off the ferry in Wrangell, Jack offered to pay for a taxi to their house, but Dan said there wasn't any. Carol said, "we left the car close by, I'll go get it you guys wait here with the bags."

Jack was impressed, he liked the town, it was kind of weather beaten looking like most seacoast towns. But he liked it.

Carol was soon back with the car. It was an old Jeep. When the three of them and all the bags were loaded there wasn't any extra space left.

As they drove off Carol said, "it's almost lunch time let's stop at the café and eat on the way home. I need to tell them I'm home anyway."

At the Café Carol had to help Dan out of the Jeep before Jack could crawl over the folded down front seat to get out. But he made it. Some people saw them coming and when they walked in the door they were greeted with a lot of enthusiasm. Jack told Dan that it was nice that these strangers were so happy to see him. Dan just laughed.

Carol told them where to sit and she went to talk to her boss while they

Looked over the menu. Jack ordered clam chowder and fish and chips, thinking that it should be fresh in this waterfront town. Carol came back with a big smile on her face and said, "eat hearty, it's on the house. Would you believe they are that glad to have me back?" Jack said, "well, let me see that menu again. If it's going to be free, I need to order more." He didn't.

It seemed like everybody in town stopped by to welcome Dan and Carol back and they introduced Jack. Everybody was very friendly. Made Jack feel right at home.

At dinner that night, Jack told them he was going sightseeing the next day. Dan said, "take the jeep and if you take me with you, I will be glad to show you the town."

"Won't Carol need the car?"

"She doesn't go to work until noon. We can come back and get her. In fact, we will have seen everything there is to see by then and she can have the car."

Dan was right, by noon they had seen everything that was to see and were back to pick up Carol in plenty of time. Jack climbed over into the back seat so Carol could drive. When they arrived at the Café

Jack bought Lunch for him and Dan and after they had eaten, he drove Dan home and took the car back for Carol and walked back to their house. It wasn't far.

When he got back, he told Dan, "I think since I've seen most of Wrangell, I will catch the boat tomorrow and go see some more country. I would like to see as many towns as I have time for before I head back.

"Well, it's been fun meeting you. I hope we see you again.

"If I don't fly back, I'll stop over on my way home. It will be a few weeks, maybe you will be ready to go back to get your peg by then and we can ride back together."

"That would be great. I hope it works out that way since I think you bought our breakfast all the way up here, and maybe I can get you to buy it all the way home too."

Carol drove him to the ferry the next morning on her way to work. After he had unloaded his gear, she hugged him and said, "I really appreciate meeting you, you have been a big help to Dan. He was down in dumps until we met you. Thank you."

"I'm glad to have met you guys too. And thanks for the hospitality. I might be stopping by again on my way home. I'll call you before I do. Dan gave me your number." He picked up his bags and waved goodbye as he walked to the ferry landing.

The next stop, Petersburg. It's on the other end of the Island just northwest of Wrangell. It's a larger town and Jack decided to spend the night there. He shouldered his backpack and picked up his suitcase and started walking up the street. He saw a sign for a Café and headed for it. As he was paying his bill after lunch, he asked the waitress, "is there a hotel in town?"

"Yes, you go up to the corner and turn left. It's down a block on the left side. It's small but nice."

"Thank you, is there a real-estate office here too?"

"Yes, just the other side of the hotel."

After thanking the waitress again, he picked up his bags and headed for the hotel. He stopped at a little store on the way and bought a paper. After checking in he went to his room and sat down at a little table and looked up the real-estate notices. He didn't plan to buy anything today. He just wanted to see what was available and the prices. He was surprised to find listings of places in Islands all around the area. He decided to go talk to the realtor.

Jack found the real-estate office two doors from the hotel. When he walked in, he saw that it was really small and bare. It had two desks and a filing cabinet and that was it. The only person there was a young Indian girl, very pretty. Jack introduced himself and the girl said, "Hi, I'm Margerate Long braid but everybody calls me Maggy. Are you thinking of settling here?"

"Yes, if I can find what I want."

"Well let me show you what we have in the book."

After the book she drove him around in her van and showed him a lot of houses. A couple of them were waterfront with boat docks and were landscaped nice and looked great. Way out of his price range though.

He said, "do you know of any that might need work or are unfinished that I might be able to afford?"

"Yes, but we will have to go by boat to see them. For a small fee my brother would take us in his boat."

"Good, what time do we meet in the morning."

"Come to my office at nine and we will go from there."

It was getting late so Jack had her drop him at the café to eat dinner. After eating he went back to the hotel and read through the real-estate listings again to find something close to what he wanted.

He had gone to bed early, so he was up early. After breakfast he walked around town for a while. The only thing open was the grocery store. He bought some snacks to take along for the boat ride. Had he known Maggie's brother he would have bought more. He was at Maggie's office at nine sharp.

When Maggy got there, she went in and got her listing book and then drove them to her house. She honked her horn then got out of the car and walked around the house and down to a boat dock where a nice boat was docked. A stocky young native American man came from the house who Maggy introduced as her brother Jim. Jack and Maggy climbed into the boat and Jim cast off and jumped in and started the engine and said, "where to?"

Maggy gave directions and they took off out around the point very fast.

Jack was so enchanted with the scenery that he wasn't as attentive to the looking at the property as Maggy thought he should be. She said, "We have looked at every waterfront listing in the book, and you haven't seemed interested in any of them."

"Too much money." Jack said. "I found some property in the paper that is closer to my price range." He took a paper from his bag of snacks that Jim had about cleaned out and handed it to Maggy. She looked at the ones he had marked and said, "they are on the Island to the west there and are for sale by owner. I can't sell them."

"I will pay you whatever your commission would be if you will take me to see them and help with the paperwork if I buy one."

She thought about it for a minute then said, "O.K. Jim, Head across the channel into the big cove over there. I know where both of those places are. I tried to get those people to list with me, but they wouldn't.

It was a very pretty boat ride of about ten minutes. What Maggy had called a big cove was miles long and a half mile wide at least. The first place they came to be a run-down little cabin with an old out house that didn't smell too good. Jack didn't think it was worth the money they were asking for it.

The second place was a new Chalet type cabin that was a long way from being done. Mostly just a shell. But it was on a little cove of its own with a little creek running into the end of the cove. Maggy showed him where some of the corner stakes were and the property lines.

After looking the place over really good, Jack told Maggy, "I like it. We need to talk to the owner. The add said he would carry a contract with a big enough down payment. That sounds good to me." They got back in the boat and headed back.

When they got back too Maggy's dock, they went up to the house and Maggy called the number in the paper. The man said he lived in Kake. A little town on the other end of the Island where the property was. He said he could come over the next day and meet them at Maggy's office.

Jack gave Jim some money for driving them around all day and asked Maggy for a ride to the café. On the way, he asked Maggy, "do you have a chart of that cove that gave the depth of the water at low tide?"

She said, "I have a chart, but I don't know about the depth information."

They went to Maggy's office, and she dug around and found the chart.

It showed the little cove, but the scale was too small to show the depth.

Jack thanked Maggy for all her help and they agreed to meet at her office at the appointed time the next day and he headed for the café for dinner.

As Jack walked down the street, he started noticing all the businesses along the way. He was looking for a chandler shop. By the time he reached the café he hadn't found one. He decided to ask the waitress if there was one in town. When he finished eating, he asked the waitress directions. She said,

"Go past your hotel and turn left at the corner It's at the end of the street by the water. But it won't be open now." Jack thanked her and headed for his hotel. He wasn't supposed to meet Maggy until ten so he would go to the chandler shop early.

In the morning Jack was at the restaurant early

for breakfast and was at the chandler shop when they opened at seven. On a board in the window was a list of boats for sale. He was looking for it over when the owner came to open the place. Jack wrote down a couple of numbers from the board and then followed the owner in. He asked to see charts of the area and was shown where to look. He found the one he wanted, and it showed the small cove that he was curious about but not the depth.

Jack went back out to look at the boat advertisements and the shop owner came out and asked, "are you looking for a boat?"

"Yes, but I need a large one I'm buying a cabin on the beach over on that Island and I am going to need one big enough to haul building materials. The place is not finished."

"I know of one that would work really good for you. It needs some work but it's cheap. When my helper gets here, I'll show it to you."

"Well, that's real nice of you but I'm not in a big hurry. I haven't bought the place yet."

Just then his helper showed up. Another Indian girl. The shop owner whose name was Mark Smith, said to the girl, "I'm taking him to the boat yard. I'll be back later."

She just nodded and went inside.

Jack said, "I feel bad about taking you away from your business."

Mark said, "it's O.K. I own a couple of those boats. If I sell you one, I'll be happy. It didn't look like we were going to be too busy at the store anyway." As they walked along the waterfront, they introduced themselves.

By the time they walked the two blocks to the boat yard they were old friends. Jack should have figured something was funny, but he didn't. It looked like the yard had about fifty boats. Everything from small speedboats to big fishing boats. Mark took him to a good-sized speedboat first. It looked to be about twenty feet long. It had a small cabin forward and was set up for sport fishing. With an open back deck. It was set up for outboards, but it didn't have any. Jack looked it over pretty good. It looked like it might work for him.

Mark said, "let me show you a bigger one."

They walked around some other boats and came to one that was kind of strange looking. It was over forty feet long, had a small cabin in the front but the rest was all open deck with a wide beam. It looked like it could haul a lot of freight. The hull was heavy aluminum that looked in good shape. Jack went up a ladder and went over the side to look over the inside. He walked forward to the cabin and found that everything had been taken out of it. It was stripped. Mark had climbed aboard and as Jack came out of the cabin he said, "I know, it needs a few things, but I will give it to you if you pay me for supplying everything for it.

Jack said, "It looks like it would about empty

your store. At first, I thought it was too much. But the more I think about it the better it looks. What about an engine?"

Mark said, "what about mounting a big outboard on it. A lot easier to come up with and when the time comes to repair?"

"And you just happen to have the right one on sale this month."

Mark said, "O.K. you got me I just could not sell this boat, so I stripped it and sold all the equipment off it. But we can get the old girl running again."

Jack took out a small notebook and a pen and started writing. Making a list of all the things the boat would need. It got to be quite a list. They headed back to Mark's shop to talk prices.

When Jack walked into Maggy's office at ten it looked like the boat was going to cost about five grand, even getting a lot of it used. Maybe the same stuff that Mark had taken out of it.

CHAPTER 3

Maggy introduced Jack to the property owner whose name was Henry Long walker. He said he was half Indian. By noon all the paperwork was done, and a check written to Maggy for a deposit. So, Henry gave Jack the keys to the place. Henry said, "It was nice doing business with you, Jack. If you come to Kake I will show you a trail through the woods to that property that you can make with a four-wheel drive truck. I hauled all the building supplies through there. You could too."

Jack said, "when I get my truck up here, I'll come look you up and thank you for the offer."

After Henry left, Jack stayed to talk to Maggy.

He said, "I was over looking at a boat in the boat yard and I think I'm going to buy it."

"I Know, the Girl in the chandler shop is friend of mine. She called me before you got here this morning."

"Yea, what did she say?"

"That it was going to cost you a lot of money to get that thing working."

"What do you think of the idea?"

"The man who used to own that boat hauled freight for people between the Islands. You could too. I don't know if it would be enough to make a living though."

"I don't need to make a living at it. I am a writer of books and have enough money coming in to live without working full time."

"I see that you are paying cash for Henry's property. Are you rich?"

"If I was, I wouldn't be buying an unfinished house and a junked boat.

"I just got an advance on a book that was just published, and I need to spend it, so I don't have to pay taxes on it. Buying property and a boat for a business will work that way. It's about lunch time can I buy lunch?"

"Sure, will it be deductible?"

While eating lunch, Maggy asked, "Are you married?"

"Yea so don't get any ideas. I know that I am very handsome but I'm old enough to be your grandpa. My wife will move up here when her job is finished. But she will buy a house in town. She would not like to live over there. And have to go everywhere by boat. She is a lot younger than me and will want to find a job in town anyway. She was a banker and will probably want that kind of job when she gets here."

Jack walked Maggy back to her office and then

headed for the chandler shop. When he got their Mark was busy with another customer, so he went to talk to the girl that worked there. She smiled when he walked up and he said,

"So, you told Maggy about me buying that piece of junk boat. Do you feel guilty?"

"I would if we weren't going to make a lot of money fixing it up for you. At least I will try and keep him from gouging you too much."

Jack thought that was funny. He introduced himself and she said her name was Susan and was happy to meet him. He thought that it seemed that everyone he met here was really friendly. He liked that.

Mark walked over and said, "I figured up the prices for everything on your list and it came to over five thousand and the labor will bring it up to about six. Shall we go ahead?"

"Yea but I have to return home so, I am leaving the money with Maggy. She will put it into an escrow account and will pay for the work after she inspects it. I don't want this to turn into a big rip off while I'm gone."

Mark looked like his feelings were hurt but Susan said, "that's a good plan. She will keep us honest. Your money will be safe."

They talked some more about the work to be done and then he went back to the hotel and called Dan and said he would be there tomorrow on the Seattle ferry. And could he stay with them again?

After breakfast he packed his bags and checked out of the hotel. The ferry didn't come until afternoon, so he went to Maggy's office. She had a paper to sign for the boat deal and he gave her a check for the six thousand.

When everything was done, he said, "You know that I couldn't have gotten everything done here without your help. I owe you a lot. I hope we will be friends forever. And when I come back, I will pay you for your time, whatever you say it's worth. It will be deductible."

Maggy gave him a hug and said, "do you want a ride to the boat?"

"No, it's a few hours until boat time. I think I will go look at the boat again."

"I'd like to see this wreck myself. Can I tag along?"

"Only if you cannot say mean things about it. You might hurt its feelings. You might try to think of a mane for her while I'm gone."

When they got to the yard, they walked around the boat looking over the hull.

Maggy said, "hold the ladder I'm going inside." She had on a rather short skirt that gave Jack a pretty good view of what she had on under it while she climbed. But she didn't seem to care so Jack didn't say anything.

Jack climbed up after her and they went forward into the cabin. She looked around and said, "Boy he really stripped this thing, didn't he? He even took the cushions off the bunks in the fo'c'sle. He will probably be selling you back the stuff he took out of here."

"Yea I had the same thoughts myself. Susan has a list of what I want back in here. I'm counting on you to see that it gets done. O.K?"

"Yes, I am looking forward to giving Mark a bad time about it."

"I know that I am asking a lot of you, But I need a couple of other things too. My wife is going to need a house in town to buy and a job. She won't be here for a few months so there is no big hurry. But if you would keep it in mind, I would appreciate it."

"No problem, are you going down the ladder first so that you can see my bottom again, or is it so you can hold the ladder for me?"

"Both, well it is a very pretty bottom. But of course, I won't look."

"Liar, but I'm glad you think it's pretty."

On the way back to the office they stopped at the chandler shop to talk to Susan. She was busy with a customer, so they looked around the shop and Jack picked up the chart of the area and a book of tides. When Susan was free Maggy told her that she had the money so they could start on the boat anytime.

Susan said, "Mark wants to sell you a Honda 80 horsepower, but we have a Evinrude 150 for less money and more horsepower."

Jack said, "you do what you think is best. I'm

sure that between you and Maggy it will work out just right. And thank you for your help."

Jack paid for the chart and tide book and Maggy and he walked back to her office. He picked up his bags and asked, "I still have time before the ferry comes, can I buy you lunch one more time?"

"Sure, I'm going to miss you taking me out to lunch while you're gone. When will you be back?"

"I'm not sure. The publisher has me signed up to do a talk show to sell some books. Then a couple of book signings. But I hope to be back in a month." By this time, they were at the café. Once they had ordered, Maggy said, "are you excited about you being on a talk show?"

"No, I always feel out of place there and I don't sound like I have anything intelligent to say. Oh well, it helps sell books and that's what pays the bills. I think I will write a book about moving up here."

"Well, there has never been a dull moment since you came to town. You bought a house, you bought a wreck of a boat, and arraigned for it to be fixed and all in a few days. I can't wait to see what's next."

Maggy drove Jack to the ferry landing and gave him a big hug and said,

"I'm going to miss you, Jack. I have a feeling we are going to be good friends."

"I hope so Maggy, I always need more friends. I hope that I haven't asked you to do too much for me while I'm gone."

"Don't worry I'll send you a big enough bill that I won't feel too used."

"That's good, it will make me feel better about it. I'll see you soon. Call me when the boat's ready. And send me a picture by E-mail. O.K."

"Sure." She said and waved goodbye as he went down the ramp to the boat.

It was a short ride to Wrangell, so Jack kept his bags with him at the rail while he watched Petersburg disappear around the Island. Jack never got tired of watching this Island scenery with the dense forest, rocky beaches, and a beach front house every once in a while. "I'm going to like it here." He thinks to himself. "I hope my wife does too."

He called Dan from the boat. He was excited to tell him and Carol about all the things that had happened in the last few days. When the ferry nosed into the landing Jack was the only passenger to get off there were a few to get on though. But the ferry didn't even tie up and it pulled right out.

Dan and Carol were waiting with the Jeep when he walked up the dock.

He hugged carol and shook hands with Dan and said, "Boy do I have a lot to tell you."

Dan said, "we have some big news too. The V.A. says I can get my new peg next week. So, if you can wait a couple of days we can ride back with you."

On the way to the house Jack gave them a run down on all that had happened since he was there last. When they were in the house, he took out his chart to show them where the house is that he bought.

Dan said, "It's too bad you couldn't find something on our Island."

Jack said, "I think that Wrangell is too small. I needed a bigger town so that I can find a job for my wife when she moves up here."

"Do you have to haul all the materials by boat to finish your house?"

"Well, the guy who sold the house to me said there is a path through the woods that a four-wheel drive truck can make. He said that he hauled all the stuff to build it with in his. I have a good old truck. But if I must do it with a boat, I just happen to have one."

Carol said, "what is her name?"

"I think I'll call her the Terry Babett. Those are my wife's nick

-names."

"Babett?"

"It's the French nick-name for Elizabeth."

Dan said, "I'm glad that we're riding back together it will be good to have the company."

Jack said, "I'm surprised that you got an appointment so quickly."

Carol said, "He bugged them every day until they

gave in just to shut him up. Are you going to stay in town for the night? Or head out for home when we land?"

"Get a room with two beds. I'll just stay with you."

"Dan snores so loud that you will not get any sleep."

"My wife snores. I'm used to it. I'll at least get a room in the same hotel. That way I can buy you dinner."

Carol said, "You have been buying us dinner since we met. We are beginning to feel like freeloaders."

"If I didn't buy you dinner you probably wouldn't eat with me. Besides I owe you for putting me up when I'm in town."

When the day came to catch the ferry, Carol drove them down to the ferry landing and Jack unloaded the bags and Carol unloaded Dan. Then she drove the Jeep to the Café and walked back. When the ferry nosed into the landing, and they lowered the ramp no cars got on or off, so Jack and Carol carried the bags on while Dan hobbled along on his crutches. The ramp went up and they backed out and were on their way.

Jack went to the purser's office and rented the biggest room they had. It had two beds. He dumped his bags on one of the beds and went and found Dan and Carol.

He asked, "did you rent a cabin?"

Dan looked embarrassed and said, "Cabin are for sissies, we'll sleep on the deck chairs."

"Well, if you decide to be sissies, I rented one with two beds you can bunk with this sissy if you want to. Would you like me to put your bags on the other bed for you?"

Carol laughed and said, all the sudden I like sissies. I will be happy to share."

Dan said, "I better come along to chaperone." They all laughed then.

Jack put their bags in his cabin and met them in what Dan called the mess hall. After lunch they went out on deck to watch the Islands slide by.

On arrival in Bellingham Jack and carol carried the bags off while Dan hobbled along behind on his crutches. As they passed through the terminal Jack said, "If you will wait here, I'll get my car. It's in a lot down the street. I won't be long. Then I will drive us to the hotel. That way you won't have to rent a car."

While he was gone Dan said, "we don't have money to rent a car we would have to take a bus. Or something."

"Don't tell Jack that or he would be trying to give us money."

"Yea, you know for an ex-Marine he's a hell of a nice guy."

"What does be an ex-Marine have to do with it?"

"Everybody knows what mean bastards they are."

When they got to the hotel the clerk told Dan that the V.A. didn't authorize a room for them until the next day.

Jack asked, "how long are you going to be here?"

Carol said, "three days."

Jack said, "I'll rent one with two beds for four days and you can just stay there. You must be used to staying with me by now. Besides I'll enjoy seeing Carol running around in her teddy one more time."

Carol said, "I don't even own a teddy."

Jack acted shocked and said, "You mean you were naked? I hope this room has lighter."

After breakfast Jack loaded up his car and after hugging Carol, he handed her a card in an envelope and said, "give this to Dan after he's done at the hospital. It's just a get-well card with one of my wonderful sentiments. See you when I get back to Alaska."

With that he jumped in his car and drove off. She opened the envelope and found three one-hundred-dollar bills in it. She took them out and put them in her purse. It was a good thing. They were going to need the money before they got home. Mean bastard hell. She won't tell Dan. Well, not for a while anyway. Not until he makes some comment about how mean ex Marines are.

CHAPTER 4

J ack was moving right along on I-90 heading east
on his way home.

He got to thinking about Dan and Carol. He felt sorry
for those two. He hoped the three bills will get them
home without starving. I think the good Lord sent me
along to help them at just the right time.

He was looking forward to getting home and
telling his wife of all that had happened in the last
couple of weeks. She was not really 6 1happy   about
moving to Alaska. Her two kids and eight grandkids
would be left behind. But maybe we could talk them
into moving up there too. Yea sure.

Last week when he called his wife, she said that she
had put the house up for sale. If it sold for anywhere
near the asking price, we would have enough to pay
cash for a house in Alaska. In the small Island towns
like Wrangell, they were reasonably priced. Not near
the bigger towns like Ketchikan though. As he got
closer to home, he began to be a little worried about
his wife not wanting to go. They had talked a lot about
the plan, and she had agreed to it. But she has said
many times that if anything happened to him, she

would sell the house and move into a condo. So that she didn't have to take care of a lawn or plow snow. Oh well quit worrying you'll be home soon and then you will know.

When he pulled into the driveway his wife came out onto the front porch to meet him. He carried his bags up onto the porch and hugged his wife. Once in the house he put his bags down and got out his chart. They sat down beside each other at the kitchen table so Jack could show her the places on the chart and tell her of his big adventure. He told her of meeting Dan and Carol and how that Dan was at that moment at the V.A. getting a new peg leg. And how he had stayed with them in Wrangell. Then how he had gone on to Petersburg, bought a house to work on and a boat to haul freight. He showed her pictures on his phone of everything.

She said, "You don't expect me to live in a house that you can only get to by boat, do you?"

"No, I know better than that. I bought it to finish and resell. I know you don't like boats."

Jack talked a long time telling her about everything that had happened.

She asked, "did you find us a house?"

"No but I think finding you a job is more important. I have a couple of people looking for that. We must have a house in the same town as you get a job. I'm hoping that it's Petersburg. It's a bigger town so more opportunity. How did things go while I was gone?"

"I watched the baby the whole weekend. So, I am ready to move away from here."

"I know, two-year-old are hard work. I think that I'm too old for it."

"You do better than I do. That little girl really knows how to push my buttons. And the teenagers all want something they are always calling me. I think I spend more on them than I do on myself."

There were a lot of things to do to get ready to move. She had to go through all the stuff in the storage room. Some of that stuff had been in there for years and not even looked at. Jack went through everything out in the shop. What they decided not to keep would go out for a garage sale. They would have to park both cars outside until after. Jack thought he would just keep what tools he needed to finish the house on Kake Island and sell the rest. Both decks needed a fresh coat of paint. So did the whole inside of the house.

When it was all done, and they got an offer on the house Jack loaded all the tools that he wanted and the furniture from his office onto his old chevy four-wheel drive truck and headed for Bellingham and the ferry.

He would need all of this stuff at the house on Kake Island. He hoped that Henry had been right about being able to drive to the house from Kake.

He was going to need a few things. For one thing he was going to need help. He could not move the furniture by himself.

When the truck was loaded on the ferry, and he

had rented a cabin he called Dan.

Carol answered. He said, "Hi Carol, Jack here I'm on the boat and on the way finally. How is Dan doing with his new peg?"

"He's doing fine now. He had a lot of pain at first, but the stump has healed now, and he is walking all over and is looking for a job. I hope he finds one soon He's driving me crazy."

"Is he home? I have a lot of stories to tell."

"No, he's out looking for work."

"Is he over being mad at me about the money I left?"

"I never told him. He would not have spent it and it made the trip better."

They talked for a while and when he hung up, he called Maggy.

When she answered he said, "Hi Maggy it's Jack, have you got some good news for me?"

"You know I used to know a guy named Jack. That was a long time ago and I haven't heard from him lately. The boat is done. It's tied up at my dock. Have you decided what you are going to name her yet?"

"The Terry Beth after my wife. Do you need more money?"

"No, we got it done for a little less than we figured. We even added a boat bailer. It rained a lot, and we were afraid it would sink. I found a job that your wife can apply for. It's for a bank manager and it will depend on her qualifications of course. Did you sell your house?"

"We got a good offer on it, so I came ahead. She will stay until it closes."

"How much are you wanting to spend for a house here?"

"What have you got?"

"I have a three-bedroom two bath with a two-car garage. It's not waterfront but it's just across the street and has access to a dock."

"That sound pretty good. How much?"

"They are asking $95000. It may sound high but it's a nice house."

"When I get to town, I'll take a look at it. Did you figure up a bill for me for all the work you are doing for me?"

"I'm keeping track of my time. You're on your way but you're not coming to town?"

"I'm going to Kake and drop off my truck at the house there. Maybe I could get your brother to pick me up there. I could use some help unloading my truck and would be happy to pay him for his help."

"I'm sure it can be arraigned, just call me and let me know when."

Next, he called Henry to arrange for him to meet the ferry so he could show him the trail to his house.

It was early summer, and he had time but he needed to get the house done before winter. That trail would probably not be good in the winter.

He went to eat dinner and then to his favorite pastime. Watching the scenery go by. It was raining so he watched through the window.

Three days later he was driving his truck off the ferry when he saw Henry. Henry waved for him to follow him and headed for a restaurant and stopped. When Jack got out of the truck, Henry said, "I haven't had lunch and it will be a while before I get back to town. I'll buy."

The town of Kake was a quaint little waterfront town very charming.

After lunch Jack told Henry, I am going to leave my truck at the house and commute by boat. A friend is going to pick me up there."

"O.K. I'll stop at my house and pick up my four-wheeler. This car would never make it."

With Henry on his four-wheeler and Jack following in his truck they went through town and right to the forest and Henry disappeared into the woods. Jack slowed down and followed. It wasn't much of a track. At places tree limbs scraped along the sides of the truck. It was a good thing that it was four-wheel drive. They finally came out into a clearing with a creek running through it. The house was just on the other side. Jim was waiting at the house to help unload the truck. Jack could see that he couldn't drive across the creek, but Henry had put a couple of two by twelve's across for a foot bridge. He turned the truck around to make it easier to unload and they got to work.

When everything was in the house, Henry gave the deed and the keys to the house to Jack and left.

Jim said, "About ready to go? I'm tired and hungry and want to go home. Besides Maggy has a big dinner for us waiting."

"I'll be a few minutes. I want to change the locks. Who knows how many people have keys?"

"You don't trust people much do you?"

"I've been a builder for a long time and a lot of people have sticky fingers."

On the way to Maggy's Jim told of taking the Terry Beth out on a test run. He said that the Evinrude motor made her clip right along. He thought it would do about twenty knots. Jack couldn't wait to see it. Jim said,

"I even painted the name on it. I'll bet it didn't go that fast with the original motor in it."

Maggy was waiting on the dock when they arrived.

She said, "You guys took long enough, dinner is ready. I thought you'd be here an hour ago.

Jim said, "He had to change the locks on the house. He said there were too many Indians around." Jack looked a little shocked.

Maggy said, "don't pay any attention to him he's

always saying things like that. And he's only a half breed."

Jack smiled and said, "Give me a minute to look over my boat I'd like to see how good a job you did before I have to pay the huge bill you have for me." They all climbed over the side and looked it over good.

Jack said, "It looks good, Maggy you did great.

After dinner Jack paid Jim for his help and Jim went to town.   Said he had a date.

Jack said, "O.K. Maggy let's see that bill you have for me." She gave it to him. It was for three hundred dollars. He wrote out a check for a thousand and handed it to her.

She said, "that is too much Jack I didn't do that much. Susan did most of it.

"You did plenty, and if it weren't for you none of it would be finished. Besides I need to pay you for dock fees and that fine dinner."

"I think you're crazy, you can leave the boat here as long as you need."

"I am going to need a small boat to go back and forth to the cabin to work. I will also need some help. What does Jim do for a job?"

"He works on a fishing boat during the season which will start soon. You might find someone at the Indian village but most of them fish too. You might get one of the girls though."

"Will they be strong enough? The work will be

hard."

"Susan has a cousin that's as big as most men, she would be strong enough. She is a rascal though she is always getting into fights with men to show how tough she is."

"That's great now you want me to get beat up by a girl who works for me.?"

"I'll talk to Susan; the girls name is Minnow, and she does need a job.

Have you got a bed and things at the house?"

"I need a lot of things. All I brought was my office furniture, but it includes a futon, a computer desk with computer, a big chair and foot stool an end table, and a couple of lamps. I will need a gas range, a generator, a water heater, a wood stove. All very heavy stuff. I also have to figure a way to get it from the boat to the shore."

Maggy drove Jack to the hotel and told him to meet her at her office at nine in the morning. That she would have Minnow there to meet him at that time.

All during the evening he thought about what to do about the boat.

What to do about loading and unloading. By morning he had a couple of ideas figured out.

He got to Maggy's just before nine and was looking at the pictures of houses that she had in the window. Then he remembered that he hadn't seen the house that Maggy wanted to show him. A girl walked up beside and stood there staring at him. He turned and looked at her she was tough looking like a weightlifter.

She smiled a little smile and said, "Hi, I'm Minnow, are you Captain Jack?"

Jack smiled and said, "No one has called me captain since I owned a fishing boat back in the seventies. But yes, I'm Jack." They shook hands. She had a good strong grip. But not like someone trying to show how strong they are. She was quite pretty for a weightlifter. Jack thought he was going to like her.

At nine, Maggy showed up. Jack said, Minnow and I have already met. And she didn't try to beat me up like you said she would. So, I think I'll hire her if she doesn't want too much in the way of wages. Hey, you were going to show me a house to buy."

On the way, Maggy stopped at the bank for a minute to deposit Jack's check. When she got back in the car, she handed jack a card and said, "tell your wife to send her résumé and picture to this person for the job at the bank. He's a dirty old man so if she's good looking he'll probably hire her even if her resume is not that great."

Jack liked the house and said, "If she gets the job, we'll take it."

Maggy said, "don't you want to dicker a little on the price?"

"My wife probably will. But I don't like to, except when it comes to wages, I like to dicker over them."

Maggy smiled at Minnow and said, "Don't worry, He will probably offer you more than you ask for."

Minnow said, "how about five bucks an hour?"

Jack said, "What is minimum wage here in Alaska?"

Minnow said, nobody pays Indians minimum wage."

Jack said, "I do, and if you are a good worker like Maggy says I'll pay you more." By then they were at Maggy's house. They wanted to show Minnow the boat. They walked around the house. When they got to where they could see the boat Minnow said, "Wow, that's a lot bigger than I thought it would be."

As they climbed aboard Jack peeked at Maggy's bottom again. Minnow had on pants, so he didn't get to see hers.

Maggy said, "Did you peek again?"

"Sure, if you don't like it stop wearing skirts. It's too much to resist."

As they looked the boat over, Jack said, "The first thing we need is a way to unload freight. I've some ideas but it's going to take some work and my tools are all over at the cabin. I need to take a quick run over there for tools."

Maggy said, "you can take my boat. It would be faster. You and Minnow can go now if you want. That way Minnow can see the house you boug ht."

The Terry Beth would be a lot slower, so they were

soon speeding over the water. When they reached the small cove Jack run the boat up on the beach and took a rope off the bow and tied it to a log stuck in the sand. Minnow climbed out over the bow, and they walked up to the cabin together.

She said, "this is a beautiful place. I am going to like working here. The setting has a lot of charm with the little cove and the creek and the cabin. It's beautiful."

"There is a lot of work to do though. We need a bridge across the creek, a dock, and to finish the cabin. It's going to take a few months."

Jack unlocked the house, and they went in. Minnow looked the place over and said, "no plumbing, no electrical, and no chimney. Are we doing all of that?"

"Yea and a wind generator for making electricity, and a garage for my truck, and a shed for gas tanks and another for batteries for the wind generator. I wonder how much snow we get here and if the creek freezes up?

Yea a lot of work. We will need help every once in a while, do you know someone who is a good worker and strong?"

"For minimum wage I know quite a few."

They loaded up with the tools he wanted and locked the place up and headed back to the boat.

When they got back to the dock, they loaded all of the tools into the cabin of the Terry Beth. Jack took a lot of measurements and then they took Maggy's boat to the dock of the chandler shop. As they walked in Susan came over and hugged Minnow and said,

"Well, did he hire you or did you beat him up?"

Minnow looked embarrassed and said, "I haven't beaten anybody up in a long time. And he did hire me."

"How long is a long time, a month?"

Jack said, "O.K. Susan, don't pick on my hired help. I need some things for that wreck you stuck me with. You did a good job on it though. Thank you." He gave her his list of equipment he wanted and asked where to get the lumber he needed.

Minnow said, "I will show you while she gets your order ready."

Just a block away was the lumber company she took him to. When they walked up to the counter in the store Minnow said, "This is Captain Jack of the Terry Beth. We need some lumber and hardware for the boat. But he has a couple of houses to finish and will want contractor discounts.

The man came from behind the counter and shook hands with Jack and said, "Nice to meet you Jack, I'm Deke Fouler, is this wild cat working for you?"

"Yea, but so far so good. I will be paying cash for everything, but I will need to open an account for when she picks things up for me." He gave the man his list and paid for it and said, "I will bring the boat around if you can see to it that the lumber is down at the dock to be loaded."

"No problem, see you when I see you."

They went back to Maggy's boat and jumped in and took it back to her dock.

Jack went aboard the Terry Beth and started the engine and while it was warming up Minnow untied it from the dock and climbed aboard. Jack backed it out into the channel and turned and headed for the lumber company dock. Minnow came into the wheelhouse and said,

"Well, how does she run? Does the big size bother you?"

"No, I used to have a fishing boat, it was almost this big. And she runs fine. They did a good job fixing it up. By the way You seem to know everybody around here. That man at the lumber company seemed to know you pretty well. How about spreading the word that we will be hauling freight around the Islands?"

"You are a writer; you should write an article for the paper telling the story of a sad old boat that was dry-docked and is now all fixed up and ready to haul freight around the world. The editor might even hire you to write a column for his paper."

"Boy, you are full of it today. Go get the fenders out and stand by to tie us up. Try to make yourself useful."

The yard boys brought the lumber to the dock on a forklift and handed it down to Minnow and him to stack in the boat. When done they moved the boat to the chandler shop and Susan and Mark helped load all the stuff Jack had ordered. Jack paid the bill and they headed for Maggy's dock. And went to work. Jack had bought a generator at the lumber company to run his power tools so by dinner time they had the work done on the boat to Jacks satisfaction. Since Maggy wasn't home yet they borrowed her boat again and went downtown to a waterfront restaurant for dinner. While eating Jack asked, "Where do you live?"

"I live in the Indian village. But since I am now among the employed, I'm going to rent a room from Susan. She lives just a few blocks from Maggy."

Jack said, "we need to buy a boat like Maggy's for running around."

Minnow said, "Are you going to run out of money with all this buying?"

"I am going to need one bigger thing. A backhoe, I need to do a lot of digging that I don't want to do by hand. It will have to be a small one that we can haul in the boat. I could haul it on the ferry to Kake and bring it through the woods. Where is the closest tractor dealer?"

"I think the biggest is in Ketchikan. You would probably get the best deal there. I'll ask around and see if anyone around here has one for sale. How soon do you need it?"

"We have to build a bridge across the creek first before we can get anything to the cabin by land."

"What do we need for that?"

"Some garden hoses and a wheelbarrow and a lot of cement bags and a skiff."

"I know a guy with a fourteen-foot fiberglass one. It doesn't look like much but it's cheap, just fifty bucks."

They were done eating so as they left the restaurant Jack gave Minnow fifty bucks on the way back to the boat. He said,

"Where is this skiff?"

"Up by Susans'. I can row it down to Maggy's in the morning. What time do you want me there?"

"The lumber company doesn't open until eight, so it won't do much good to be there before then."

When they got back to Maggy's she was home. Jack went to her house to talk to her. He said, "I need a boat like yours to go back and forth to the cabin. I plan to anchor the Terry Beth in the cove over there and leave it until I need it. It's too slow to run back and forth all the time. And thank you for letting me use yours all this time."

"You're welcome, Jack. There are always boats for sale in these Islands. It just depends how much you want to spend. You should ask Susan she knows about most of them. How is Minnow working out?"

"She is doing fine; I like her spirit. But she never wears skirts, so I don't get to see her bottom."

"If you asked her, she would probably show you.

She is a rascal. And so are you."

She offered him a ride to the hotel, He said thank you, but he would walk. It was a nice night, and he would like a stroll.

The morning found Jack at the dock at seven doing some work on the boat. About seven thirty he heard something bump alongside and a yell.

He walked out of the cabin and looked over the side to see Minnow in an old green Sears Game fisher. She said, "Throw me a rope there is nothing to tie it on with. He threw her a rope and walked to the rear end and tied on the other end. Then put a ladder over for her. She handed up the oars and climbed aboard.

"Any trouble?" He asked.

"No, well I had to threaten to beat him up to get the oars. Sometimes it pays to have a bad reputation."

Jack just smiled and thought about what Maggy had said about Minnow showing him her bottom. He just shook his head and started the engine. He thought about telling Minnow to cast off, but he looked out the window and saw that she was doing it.

When they tied up to the lumber company dock. They weren't open yet, so they walked over to the chandler shop to see Susan. After they all hugged, Jack said, "We need a boat like Maggy's to go back and forth to the cabin. She said to ask you. I'm running out of money, so it needs to be cheap."

"There is one tied up at the boat yard dock for

four hundred. It's old but the engine runs well. It should get you back and forth O.K. if you are going to look at it don't take Minnow with you, she beat the guy up once if he knew she was with you he probably wouldn't sell it to you. I've got the keys to it. Go look at it, if you like it just run it back here and I'll take care of the paperwork for you."

Jack left an angry Minnow with Susan and went to look at the boat. He was back in about five minutes driving it. He tied it up and went up to the shop and paid Susan the money for it and then bought some cushions that doubled as life jackets for the seats were just wooden benches. He bought a large gas can too. And some two-cycle oil. He also bought two long range handhelds C.B. radios since there was no service at the cabin for his cel-phone. Mark had a C.B. with a long antenna set up at the store to use in case of emergency.

They loaded what they got from Susan into the new old boat and drove it over to the Terry Beth and tied it on.

At the lumber office, they saw Deke and Jack gave him his order. Then went around and picked up other things he needed. He told Minnow to get some gloves that fit. Get two pair. Jack paid for everything, and they went to the boats to wait for the yard boy to bring the stuff. They stopped for lunch on their way out.

While eating Minnow asked, "what are you going to name the new boat?"

"I think we'll call it the Minnow after the one on Giligan's Island.

She laughed and said, "won't your wife get jealous?"

"I'll tell her it's yours.

When they pulled into the cove Jack told Minnow to throw an anchor off the stern and start letting out line. He pulled way up into the cove, and she dropped off the bow anchor and started letting out line. Jack kept to one side of the rear line while he backed up. He yelled out the window for her to tie off the bow line. He shut off the engine and went out and started pulling in the stern line until both lines were tight. And they were just about in the middle of the cove with about twenty feet to either shore. The tide was in so when it went out the boat would drift. He would have to figure something out for that.

They used the new boom to lift the pallet of cement and tools off into the Minnow. When the boom swung over the side the boat leaned over, but not too bad. Minnow run the Minnow alongside the beach and Jack rowed the skiff to the beach. They carried everything up above the high-water mark and left it. Jack took the pipe and fittings and hose and started up the hill.

Minnow said, "What do you want me to do?"

"Load the cement bags into the wheelbarrow and take them to where we will build the bridge. Then make sure that the Minnow is not sitting in the mud when we want to go home."

Jack strung the hoses out from where the bridge was going up along the creek until he ran out of hose. Then waded into the creek and moved some rocks to make a small pool. He cut the pipe and glued on the fittings so that the hose could be connected. After connecting the hose, he laid the pipe in the creek and put some rocks on it to hold it down. Now he had running water. He took the rest of the pipe and fixed it up with a shut off valve and fittings to hook the hose to. He told minnow to start hauling sand from the beach to make cement with. While he started hauling rocks. All morning they worked at it. When Minnow said, "Hey Jack, would you like some lunch? I brought enough for two since you don't have a mama to make one for you."

Without looking up he said, "I thought Indians were supposed to be silent. What happened to you?" He then looked up. She had stripped down to shorts and a tank top and no bra.

She said, "Well, I got hot. If you don't like what you see, don't look."

He couldn't help but look, she wasn't hiding much. They went into the house to eat away from the bugs.

After lunch Jack showed Minnow how to mix mortar. He showed her how to work the shut off valve on the hose. And he started laying the stone to build the abutment for the bridge.

She said, "Why shut the water off? Why not just let it run back into the creek?"

"We don't want to wastewater, you know, waste not want not."

"You are nutting the creek runs all the time."

"When you have some spare time, start hauling rocks on the other side."

"Spare time, He says."

"Don't mumble, it's not polite."

"Working for you, maybe minimum wage is not enough."

He just smiled and kept laying stone.

By quitting time, they had one side done. They locked the tools back in the house. And headed for the Minnow.

Jack said, "If you put your clothes back on, I'll buy you dinner."

"What? You don't like the way I look?"

"Oh yea, but if you go into a restaurant looking like that you'll start a riot. You look too good. At least put on a shirt. With your tank top wet like that you aren't hiding much."

With the wind and the spray of crossing back to town, she was happy to put her shirt back on.

While eating dinner, she asked, "do you have any kids?"

He said, "Two boys and two girls and a dozen grand kids."

"What do they do for jobs?"

"The oldest son is a builder like me. The other son is in the Army. The oldest daughter is a massage person. The younger one works in a bank."

"Are the boys married?"

"Are you looking for a husband?"

"Aren't all single girls?"

"The older one is divorced."

"How old is he and is he good looking like you?"

"He's taller than me but almost as good looking. He's forty-five."

"That means he's twenty years older than me."

"Aren't there any young men around here that are willing to put up with your meanness?"

"I guess not I'm not married."

When they left the restaurant Jack told Minnow to take the boat home with her and to pick him up at the lumber company in the morning. He liked that you had to do everything by boat. When he got to his hotel room, he checked his phone messages and the E-mail. One E-mail from his publisher. Book sales are doing good. When will the next one be done? Good luck he hadn't written a line since he got here. He called his wife to see how things are going. She said, "The house closes in two weeks. Did you find one that you like up there?"

"Yea, did you send your résumé to the bank?"

"Yes, they called me and said come to work. Sounds like they are desperate."

"What kind of picture did you send? Not that one from Hawaii I hope."

"Very funny. I can't find a decent priced moving company. What should I do?"

"Have some moving company haul everything down to the pier in Seattle and I'll pick it up with my boat."

"Is your boat that big?"

"Yes, you will have to arrange with the port of Seattle where to do the loading at. Then call me and I will be waiting when they get there."

When Jack left the lumber company, he found Minnow waiting for him at the dock where he loaded an Ice chest and a bundle of wedges into the boat. And they left. On the way to the cabin he said, "I need to be gone for about a week. I am going to Seattle in the Terry Beth to pick up my furniture. Do you want to come along? It would save time. You could help with the driving."

"Are you kidding, I would love to go. I haven't been to Seattle in years.

"We are not going to have time for a shopping spree. We need to get in and out quickly. We will have to get the boat ready to go. There are no dishes or pots and pans or food. Can you cook?"

"Yes, I'm a good cook, I will make out a shopping

list for food."

"Nothing fancy now we only have a two-burner stove. And no fridge."

"I know a lot of soup recipes. What are the sleeping arrangements?"

"There are two bunks down below. We each get one, one of us will have to be at the wheel all the time anyway."

At noon the other abutment was done. After lunch they cut down a couple of birch trees to make logs for the bridge. To support the concrete.

They quit early to shop for the trip. Jack brought the blankets from the fu-ton for his bed on the boat.

That night Jack's wife called him and said, "The moving truck will be at the dock by six o'clock P.M. five days from now can you make it by then"

"We will leave in the morning, just in case we run into trouble we should have plenty of time."

"We? Who is going with you?"

"On a long trip it takes two people to run the boat. I can't make a three-day trip without some sleep."

When he hung up, he called Susan and told her to pass the word to Minnow that we were going to leave in the morning. To bring everything for the trip. He spent the evening going over the charts to decide the route through the Islands that he wanted to take. Then he called Maggy.

He said, "Hi, do you think we could get the house in a week? My wife will be here in a week, and she will want to start changing things before she moves in. You know like the paint and carpet and move the garage to the other side of the house. I don't know what all.

Maggy laughed and said, "I'm sure it will be O.K. When is the furniture coming?"

"We are leaving in the morning. We are going to get it in the Terry Beth. If we don't spend too much time goofing off down there, we should be back in a week or so. But we will have to leave it on the boat until she gets the house the way she wants it. She will want to hire someone to help her paint and clean and such. Can you help with finding someone for her?"

"Yes, in fact Minnow has a sister who would love to make minimum wage like her sister."

"Minnow now says that I work her too hard for minimum wage."

"You watch out for her I think she is starting to fall for all your charms."

"You have to be kidding I'm old enough to be her grandpa. In fact, I have grandkids her age."

"she says you don't act old. She says she has never seen anyone work as hard as you do."

"She is a good worker too. We'll, see you when we get back. I gave my wife your number so you can expect a call when she gets here. By."

As soon as he hung up, he thought about Minnow getting a crush on him and called his son Eric and when he answered he said, "I am on the way down there in my new boat and should arrive in three days to pick up a load of freight. How about taking a couple of weeks off and ride back up with me and we'll do some fishing? I know where there are some monsters lurking beneath the waves just waiting for you." And he thought 'a pretty girl too.'

"On the surface that sounds pretty good, Dad. But I know you and you Probably have some big job you want me to do while I'm there."

Jack cut him off with, "No just fishing, I have been working too hard and need some time off too."

"You never take time off. But I will take a chance because I love fishing. But I swear, if you are trying to pull a fast one I will fly home the day I get there."

"I promise, No fast ones. Not even a slow one. Don't forget a pole with heavy line these are big fish."

In the morning Minnow picked up him and his bags and they headed for the Terry Beth with a boat load of stuff. When they arrived, they tied to the big boat and unloaded the stuff from the Minnow into the Terry Beth and tied the Minnow and the skiff to the buoy that they had placed there for that reason. Jack started the engine, and they pulled the anchors and backed out of the cove. Now they were on the first long trip in the boat. Both were excited. While Minnow stowed all their junk they had brought, Jack told her about Eric coming back with them. And about Eric being suspicious of his motives.

She said, "I am a little suspicious too. What are you up to Jack?"

"Here I am always innocent of any wrongdoing, and you are insinuating something evil. I'm shocked."

"Now I'm sure that you are up to something." He told her to take the wheel and called Dan.

When Dan answered, Jack said, "Hi Dan it's your only friend Jack. How's the new leg doing?"

"I'm getting used to it. How are things going with all of your projects?"

"Things are good. We are on our way to Seattle, and I thought we would stop at Wrangell to top off our gas tanks we should be there in about twenty minutes. Maybe you could come down and see the boat if you have time?"

"No problem, I don't have any bells to put on, but I'll be there anyway. What's the name of the boat so I'll know what to look for?"

"The Terry Beth. It looks like an outhouse on the end of a raft You won't miss it."

"I can't wait to see it. O.K. See you soon."

When they tied up to the fuel dock in Wrangell, sure enough here came Dan limping down the dock with a big smile on his face. After the hand shaking and hugging of Minnow. They sat in the cabin and talked while

CHAPTER 5

Minnow filled the gas tanks and cans and secured everything. When all was ready, Dan shook hands with Jack and hugged Minnow again and Minnow cast off the lines and they were off on the way.

Minnow said, "Boy he sure likes to hug. He acts like we were old friends."

"Some girls are built just right for hugging. And if there was some kind of contest you would win."

"What does that mean?"

"That you have a great figure. How about making some lunch?"

The Islands slid by, they saw a pod of killer whales, they passed a ferry going the other way. They passed tugboats towing barges full of freight going north. And others going south towing log rafts down to the mills in the south. When it started getting dark, they turned on the running lights and a big spotlight on the roof of the cabin so they could see the channel markers out ahead of them. Jack told Minnow to go to bed. That he would wake her up in four hours. Then he would get some sleep. He didn't wake her up. After she had slept six hours she came up from below and said, "You didn't wake me. Why?"

"I wasn't sleepy." He reached up and shut off the big spotlight. It was getting light already. Light enough to see without the light anyway.

Minnow made some breakfast and after they ate Jack went below for a nap. He slept for five hours and when he came up and took over the wheel, Minnow made lunch. The coffee pot was on the little stove and Jack pored himself a cup and then took a bite of the sandwich that Minnow handed him.

It was smoked fish on homemade bread. Jack said, "This is really good. What kind of dressing is that on it?"

"Just something I make. It goes good with fish. Fish is the main food at the Indian village. So, we have invented lots of ways to fix it. Wait until you taste my fish stew."

"I can hardly wait."

They took turns at the wheel until almost dinner time. Then Minnow peeled potatoes and sliced them into a pot and started them cooking on the stove She added some veggies and a lot of pieces of smoked fish and spices and herbs. It smelled good. Boy, poor Eric, he didn't have a chance. He liked to eat. And this girl was not only pretty. She could cook.

Jack called Susan and said, "Susan sweetheart would you get someone to take one of those smokers with the separate stoves over to the house we just got and set it up in the back yard with a supply of wood for it. My son is coming back with us, and he loves smoked fish, and he will want to catch them himself. Minnow can show him how to smoke them.

It was noon the next day before they arrived at the Seattle wharf. Jack pulled in right next to Ivars restaurant and tied up. He wasn't sure that it was O.K. But that was where they were to meet Eric. He decided to stay there until someone told him to leave.

He shaved and put on a clean shirt his pants and boots looked good enough. The tide was down some, and you couldn't reach the deck of the patio, so Jack hooked the ladder up there that they used to get down into the skiff. It would work. Minnow came up from below in a nice blouse and a skirt and flat shoes. She looked good. She climbed up onto the rail and said, "hold the ladder Jack, it's not to stable. And no peeking."

But when she reached the top of the ladder and climbed over the rail everybody in the restaurant saw her panties.

A waitress showed them to a table and gave them menus. They were only there a few minutes when Eric showed up. His two girls were with him.

Haley was the oldest. And Ellen the younger. Jack introduced everybody and hugged everybody, and they were all surprised to find out about Minnow. Jack said, "Do you expect me to run a boat down here by myself? It's a three-day trip. Besides she works for me all the time. She's a good worker."

Eric said, "And good looking, no guys available, or at least an ugly girl. What does your wife think about this?"

Minnow said, "The guys all work the fishing boats during the season. And I'm the strongest girl around. His wife had to hire a girl to help her too."

During lunch the granddaughters asked Minnow a lot of questions about Alaska. They had never met an Indian girl before and they just wanted to hear her talk. Jack and Eric talked about fishing.

Eric asked Minnow, "Are the fish as big as Dad says or is he just blowing smoke?"

She said, "you are going to need a big pole and a strong back to bring them in."

"You saw my pole. Don't you think that will be big enough?"

She just laughed and said, "I had one like that when I was six."

They all laughed then.

After lunch Jack paid the bill and he and Eric went down to the boat and the girls went shopping. Jack told Minnow to be back in an hour. That they couldn't stay tied up there for much longer. Eric told Haley to pick him up at the airport in two weeks. He'd call her.

Eric inspected the boat carefully. He said, "This old boat wasn't set up for an outboard. What kind of engine did it have?"

"It had an old Budda diesel. The outboard has much more power. I have to keep it down or It will exceed the hull speed which is about twelve knots."

"Are we going fishing off of this boat?"

"It depends on how many fish you want to ketch. I have a couple other boats. A sixteen-foot speedboat and a fourteen-foot skiff."

They were sitting in the wheelhouse drinking a beer when Minnow called. She said, "Ahoy the old scow, come help a lady."

Jack said, "go hold the ladder for her, it's kind of shaky."

Eric went out on deck and Minnow said, "Here ketch these packages. And then hold that old ladder."

Eric handed her packages in to Jack and then held the ladder for her. She knew he was looking when she went over the rail and down the ladder. The rascal planed it that way.

She went down below and came up again in shorts and sneakers.

Jack told her to cast off and started the engine. When she yelled that they were clear he backed out. Once clear of the pier he turned and headed toward the cargo wharfs. There was a lot of traffic to dodge around the wharfs, ferries, big ships, and a lot of pleasure crafts too. They had all afternoon to wait for the freight, so they went and found a fuel dock and topped off their tanks.

As soon as they were tied to the dock where they were to meet the truck, Jack went to the office and paid for the Crain time and dock fees. Back at the boat they set up lawn chairs and Jack asked Minnow to tell Eric the stories about the Raven and her people. Jack had heard them before, But the way she told them was better. And it helped to pass the time.

By the time the truck got their Minnow had some pallets set up to receive the freight. The pallets would keep the furniture up off the deck in case some water splashed over the side in sloppy weather. They got the big tarp and tie down lines and straps ready. The furniture was all in crates, so the Crain operator just lowered them down onto the pallets and they covered them and tied them down and they were ready to go.

CHAPTER 6

——◇——

Once they were started north Eric climbed up on the roof of the cabin with his lawn chair to watch the scenery and all the boat traffic. As soon as they were under way Minnow started cooking dinner. Her very tasty fish stew. When it was ready, she went out on the deck and asked if Eric wanted to eat up there. He said he would come inside. It looked like it might start raining. When he walked into the wheelhouse he said, "Wow, something smells good."

Jack said, "I farted."

Minnow said, "Nasty old man, the food even tastes good too."

She dished some up for him and some for herself and they started eating.

Eric looked up at her and said, "This is the best tasting thing I ever tasted. You're real pretty and you can cook, and you're not married. Have you ever been married?"

"No, Jack says that I'm so mean that nobody would want me. If you are asking me to marry you, I except."

"I need to sample some more of your cooking

before I decide.

When she finished eating, she dished up a plate for Jack and took over the wheel.

As soon as he was done eating, he went below for a few hours' sleep. Before he had to take the night watch.

Eric asked minnow if he could take the wheel for a while.

She said, "Do you see that buoy out there on the right?"

"Yes."

"Stay to the left of it. See the one way over on the left?"

"Yes."

"That is the other side of the channel. We need to slowly work over toward it. I'll clean up the dinner stuff while you steer. Don't run into anybody."

Eric was still at the wheel when Jack came up from below. It was raining and getting dark. Jack got out his charts and picked out an uninhabited little bay and pulled in and Minnow put on her rain gear and went out and dropped the hook. Jack got out a cot from storage and set it up in the wheelhouse and rolled up in a blanket and went to sleep. So did everyone.

Minnow was up first, making breakfast, Jack was out checking the load when Eric came up from below.

He said, "What's for breakfast?"

Minnow said, "In the Marines it's called shit on a shingle. But this is made with smoked fish instead of beef. I hope you like it." She toasted a lot of homemade bread on a little toaster over the open flames on the two-burner stove while the sauce was cooking. Then put on the coffee pot.

Jack came in and hung up his rain gear. Eric said, "How is it out there?"

"It's letting up. But I think we're in for a blow. We will hit the open sea about noon. If it's bad, we'll hold up somewhere until morning. It should be good by then. I've seen storms where the seas were thirty feet high. I don't want to go through that with this load."

Minnow dished up some food for Eric and gave him a cup of coffee. He tasted it and said, "you did it again Minnow, this is really good. You should write a cookbook."

"I can't spell. But it's a good idea I have a lot of good recipes."

"Dad can't spell, and he writes books for a living."

"Yea, but his stories are great. If you don't believe me, just ask him."

When they reached Port Hardy the waves were already between ten and twelve feet high, so Jack pulled in and they dropped the hook in the bay there.

Eric said, "show me on the chart where we are."

Jack took out the chart and showed Eric where they were.

He said, "As you can see, we are almost to the open sea. When the wind slacks off, we have fifty miles of open sea to cross before we get behind Islands again. If we were running empty, I'd go ahead. It's something to see when the seas break clear over the cabin and the boat bailer can't keep up and you have to put someone on the pumps."

Eric decided to try fishing, since they were stuck here all afternoon.

Minnow gave him some smoked fish for bait and set up two lawn chairs and brought him a beer then sat with him and watched.

It wasn't long before he hooked into something big. He was having a hard time getting it up. A half hour later Minnow got a long-handled gaff hook and leaned over the side to gaff the big flounder. But she couldn't lift it into the boat. Eric had to help her. Jack stood in the door of the cabin watching.

He didn't think she was fooling anyone. He had seen her lift heavier things than that. She just wanted Eric's arms around her.

The fish probably weighed twenty pounds. Minnow went right to work on it. She got out a board that hooked to the side of the boat and started filleting the fish. Jack set up a small gas barbeque unit and heated it up.

When she had the two fillets cut off, she threw the

rest overboard.

Eric said, "You sure waste a lot."

"The crabs have to eat too. Don't let the sea gulls get at this."

She went into the cabin and returned with a big pan and started mixing a lot of sauce to marinate the fish in. She cut the fillets into pieces and dipped them into the sauce and then put them on the barbeque. She brushed more sauce over them while they cooked. She turned the heat down and put the cover on the barbeque and went into the cabin. She told Eric to turn them over in about ten minutes and after he turned them over to brush some more sauce on them and to turn off the grill after ten more minutes.

Jack set up a card table and chairs and rounded up some beers. Then took a bucket with a rope tied to it and through it over the side and hauled in some water and washed the board that she had done the fish on and put it away.

Soon Minnow brought out a platter of fried potatoes cooked with onions and butter. Then reappeared with plates and silver wear. Jack said a nice prayer, thanking God for a nice fish and a good cook. Amen.

While eating, Eric said, "You did it again Minnow. That's great sauce."

She said, "it's the fresh fish. I mean you can't get it any fresher."

In the morning the wind had died and after

breakfast Jack started the engine, Eric pulled the anchor, and they headed out.

By dark they were halfway to Ketchikan. Jack took over the wheel during the night and by one the next afternoon they went by Ketchikan. Jack decided not to stop. Too many cruise ships there. He called Dan and said,

"How is the peg doing?"

"Doing better, I can walk almost normal. When are you getting back?"

"We will be there by dinner time. Do you want to meet us at the café for dinner?"

"Yea, sure, Carol is off tonight, and we would be happy to let you buy us dinner. What time?"

"At five. My son came back with us so save us a table."

"O.K. See you then."

Jack then called Maggy and said, "Dear sweet Maggy, would you do me a big favor?"

"What favor?"

"Would you bring my wife to Wrangell for dinner tonight? I want you and her to meet some friends of mine there. My son came back with us so she will probably want to see him."

"Sure Jack, What time?"

"We are meeting at the restaurant there at five. I'll call her and arrange it with her. I really do appreciate it. See you then."

He called his wife and told her what was going on and asked how the painting and cleaning was going.

She said, "We should be done tomorrow night. When will the furniture be here?"

"I could have it there tomorrow night. But we are going to need help. Someone with a truck. We'll have to ask Maggy."

"What would we do without Maggy?"

They pulled up to the city dock at Wrangell at four fifty. And while Minnow was tying the Terry Beth to the dock Maggy and Terry showed up.

Jack hugged his wife and said, "You haven't seen the boat yet. What do you think?"

"A lot bigger than I thought. Is that our furniture under the tarp?"

"Yea, but don't tell Eric. He'll think I got him to come back with me just to help us move."

Eric walked up then and hugged Terry and introduced her to Minnow as first mate of the Terry Beth.

Terry said, "I want you to meet Maggy our best friend in Alaska. She helps us find houses and people to help us paint them and help us move. And even brings me here in her boat. She is a sweetheart."

Eric said, "Help you move huh? I knew the old man was up to something. Just a fishing trip he says. I should have known better."

As they were walking to the café Dan and Carol came to meet them. Jack did the introductions all around. Then told how he had met them on his first trip up here. That they were his oldest friends in Alaska. He said,

"Why I've known them for three months now."

After dinner Dan and Carol walked them down to the dock. To say goodbye. Eric decided to ride home with Terry and Maggy. And they all took off. It was after dark when they anchored in the cove at the cabin and climbed into the Minney. The new name for the speed boat. And headed for home.

When Minnow dropped him off at the city dock. She said, "would you mind having an Indian for a daughter in law?"

"He would want to take you home with him and I would have to find someone else to work for me. But I would love having more grandchildren."

When he got to his hotel room, Eric was asleep in the other bed. Jack took his shaving kit and went in to take a shower. After a week of bird baths in sea water he was looking forward to a real shower.

After breakfast, Minnow picked them up at the dock and headed for the cabin. When she pulled into the cove, she ran the boat up on the sand and shut off the engine and climbed over the bow with a long line to tie to a tree above high-water line. Eric and Jack climbed out and started walking toward the cabin.

Eric said, "Whose place is this?"

Minnow said, "Jack bought it to fix up to sell. We just started working on it and Terry decided to move up here. I'll show you around, and then we'll go fishing. Jack bought a new smoker that you and I will break in."

"Are you so sure we'll catch fish?"

"I know where all the big ones are. We will need a bucket full of sauce to brush on them before we smoke them. I also know how to package them for you to ship home. But I will cook some to eat here too."

As they looked through the house Minnow told Eric all the things that needed to be done. Eric said, "I figured Dad had some plan to make me work up here."

Jack came in just then and said, "I have to take my truck to the ferry. Minnow will take you fishing and baby-sit you until tonight. See you tonight."

Eric turned to Minnow and said, "It's a good thing he didn't ask me to work. I was ready to tell him where to shove it."

"No, He told me to take you fishing and I want to show you some real fishing. We need to stop at the Terry Beth to get our poles and some bait."

Minnow knew just where the reef was. There are always big fish that hang around the reef. She dropped the anchor up from the reef and let the boat drift back with the tide until they were right over the reef. The first fish he hooked into was a thirty-pound cod. It took him a while to land it. But he was so excited about it that Minnow was laughing at him, but he didn't care.

He said, "I have never caught anything this big before."

She said, "We could hook him on for bait and catch a real big one."

She decided to try and caught a fifteen-pound red snapper almost as soon as she threw her line in.

Then Eric caught a sea bass about twenty pounds.

He said, "Does this go on forever?"

"These are just the babies. The Mamas and Papas are down there too but they are harder to catch. And they won't fit in the smoker."

"You know the old saying. Are all liars' fishermen, or are all fishermen liars?"

"That applies to the men only. I never lie."

"Did you bring that bucket of sauce? I would like to see that new smoker of Dads."

She went through to the bow and pulled in the anchor. The boat was now drifting, and she started the engine. She let it idle for a bit and then looked to make sure Eric was ready and took off. She told Eric to clean the fish while she drove. That there was no place to do it at the dock. She drove right to the dock across the street from Jack's house and tied up. They took their fish and went across the street and around to the back yard. There was an old wooden table probably left there by the previous owners. She put her fish on it and went and knocked on the back door. Terry answered.

Minnow asked, "Do you have a garbage bag we can have? We need to get some fish ready for the smoker."

Terry said, "Sure, I didn't know we had a smoker. I wonder when that got here?"

"Jack bought it while we were in Seattle. He wanted it set up by the time we got back so we could smoke some of Eric's fish for him."

Terry had paint splatter all over her. She came out to see the fish.

When she saw them, she said, "Wow Eric those are huge."

"She says that they are the babies."

"Do you remember that little poem about a fisherman? It goes,

The fisherman, He rises early in the morning great are his preparations,

He returns late at night smelling of strong drink and the truth is not in him."

Eric said, "Minnow says that only applies to men. She never lies."

"Well, she told the truth about the fish being big. Are you going out again tomorrow?"

"If she'll take me. She knows right where they are at."

Minnow said, "Jack told me to take him fishing as often as he wanted to go. So, I guess it's up to him."

Terry said, "where is my little husband anyway?"

"He is bringing his truck over here to haul furniture tomorrow. He should be here soon. He is coming on the ferry."

At that moment Jack was on the phone with Susan.

He said, "I could use some help tomorrow. Is there a moving van in town? If not a couple of guys with a truck. The tide will be high at ten in the morning, and I can swing the crates right onto the dock at the lumber company and the forklift can set them right into the trucks. We can break them down at the house."

"I will get someone, how is Minnow working out?"

"Just fine, But I'm afraid she is falling for my son. I don't object, but he is a slow mover. I think her cooking is winning him over, but I will hate to lose her."

"Yea, me too. She is my best friend and my cousin."

"Well, the ferry is about to land. Don't forget at ten in the morning at the lumber company dock. Goodbye."

In the morning, Minnow picked up Jack and Eric at the town pier and they went to get the Terry Beth. Eric helped get the anchors in and Jack started the motor and backed out of the cove and headed for town.

Jack said, "I thought you two were going fishing."

Eric said, "Minnow said the fish will still be there after we help your dad move. So here we are. Besides I don't see how you could get in the anchors by yourself."

Minnow came in then and said, "You'd be surprised what this old man can do by himself. But he will need help with unloading. It's a good thing you're along it works better with three people."

They arrived at the dock early and tied up so that the crates could swing over onto the dock with ease. They started unloading. At ten the other truck showed up. It was a flatbed and with Jack's truck they could make it in one trip. The forklift came and loaded the crates and with Eric driving Jack's truck they moved out. Jack and Minnow took the Terry Beth to the dock by his house and tied up and went up to help unload the trucks. They took crow bars and hammers to open the crates.

When everything was placed in the house where Terry wanted it. Jack paid the flatbed driver and his helper and Minnow and Eric and he carried the pieces of the crates down and threw them into the boat. Then left for the cabin. When the Terry Beth was anchored

Minnow and Eric took Jack back to town and went fishing. Jack went home and helped Terry move the furniture around to suite her. Then he made the bed and laid down and took a nap. Come on he's seventy-two.

Right away Eric caught a fish over twenty pounds. Then he looked at Minnow and said, "How about one of those big ones you were talking about?"

"Do you think I say which fish is to bite? Here put this hoochie on and cast over there. When your sinker hits the reef start reeling. I can't tell how big a fish will bite but you'll catch something." Sure, enough he hooked into a cod that was over thirty pounds. It took him a half hour to get it up to the boat. Minnow took his pole, and he gaffed the fish and drug it into the boat. He conked it on the head and sat down to rest. He looked over at Minnow and said, "Do you know where all the big ones are?"

"Of course, how would I make it as a fishing guide otherwise?"

"How about if we go smoke these two. Here takes a picture of me and these fish. I want to send it to my son."

She made him clean his fish before they left.

They tied up at the dock across the street from Jack's house and Eric carried his fish to the back yard. Jack brought out a garbage bag and laid it on the table and Minnow worked on the fish while Eric started the fire in the stove.

Jack and Eric sat in lawn chairs and drank beer and kept the fire going on the smoker. Minnow went in the house and told Terry that Jack wanted her to make his favorite fish stew dish. Was that O.K? Yes, she was tired from moving and didn't feel like cooking anyway.

At dinner, Jack said, "Susan said there was a gas thing to put in the smoker, so you didn't have to keep the fire going."

Minnow said, "It works but the fish doesn't taste the same. It's better with a wood fire."

"Yea, you aren't the one watching the fire."

"Big baby, when you want to go to bed, stoke up the fire with big pieces through in extra hickory chips and damp down the stove. By the time the fire is out the fish will be smoked."

With an angry look Jack said, "Big baby, huh?"

Terry said, "Oh shut up Jack anybody could have figured that out. Tomorrow I have to start work. I have training for two weeks, but then I'm on my own."

Eric said "you've been doing Banking forever. Are you worried about something?"

"Yes, that dirty old man's doing the training."

Minnow said, "Have Eric and Jack stop by to say hello, the first day. These two would scare a grizzly bear into an early hibernation."

Terry said, "What my two little boys?"

Minnow said," What, little. Jack is six one and

two hundred and thirty pounds and Eric is six three and two hundred and fifty pounds. Around here that's scary. I think the two of them could whip the whole town."

"Maybe, but they are a couple of teddy bears."

"You can't tell that by looking." Minnow said.

When the bank opened Eric and Jack went in together. Eric to cash some travel checks and Jack to open an account. Minnow was there too to watch. She went up to the window with Eric and said, "Take good care of him his Mama is the new manager."

Eric said, "she is my stepmom, not my Mama. The guy waiting in the other line is her husband."

When Jack stepped up to the window he said, "I would like to open a new account."

The teller said, "Only the manager does that. If you would step over to her desk, she will help you with that."

Jack walked over to Terry's desk and stood there until the man training her looked up, he said, "can we help you with something?"

Terry looked up from what she was doing and said, "Bob, this is my husband, Jack. What do you want Jack?"

"I want to open a new account. Here is a check to open it with."

She told him to sit down and filled out the paperwork and passed it to him to sign. Bob looked at it and when he saw the amount, he grabbed the check and looked at it to make sure it was good. He said, "Ten thousand?"

Terry said, "It's a cashier's check. It's good. He probably has another one in his pocket. He's just showing off."

Bob's eyes were very big, and he was having a hard time breathing. No one had ever opened an account at this bank for that much money before.

Minnow and Eric came over, they had heard the conversation and were both smiling.

Minnow said, "You don't need to worry about Him Bob, He just paid cash for two houses and three boats. I would think his check is good."

Her and Eric left the bank and when they got outside Eric said,

"That poor guy might have a heart problem now. You were pretty hard on him."

She said, "he's a jerk. I don't know anybody who likes him. He thinks he's better than anyone because he has money. I was just taking him down a notch."

"I think it was more like two or three notches."

CHAPTER 7

In the morning, Jack and Eric loaded rebar and tie wire into the truck to

take to the cabin for the bridge. Then Minnow took Eric out to go fishing.

Jack took the truck to the ferry to take to Kake Island to work on the bridge. When he got to the bridge, he found that Minnow and Eric had come and unloaded the crate material off the Terry Beth and hauled it up to the bridge. It was getting to be late when he got there. What with the ferry not getting there until after noon? But he was tying rebar when Minnow came to pick him up to go home for the night.

Eric had caught more fish and wanted to get home to smoke them.

The next day the cement truck came through the woods from Kake.

Eric and Minnow came with Jack to help pour the cement.

Minnow in rubber boots, short shorts, and a tank top. She looked great with her long hair in a braid that hung to her belt. Eric was having a hard time keeping his mind on the work. The truck didn't get there until noon. But they had rebar to tie. Minnow was good at it and she seemed to always be turned toward Eric. She had smoked fish sandwiches for them for lunch that they ate before the truck came.

When they were done with the cement, Eric helped Jack cover it with a tarp while Minnow cleaned the tools.

In the boat on the way home, Eric asked Minnow, "what do you put in the sauce on those sandwiches? They are good. They are almost as good to eat as you are to look at."

Jack said, "I think she would rather freeze on the way home than cover up anything that you might want to stare at."

Minnow said, "You were looking too."

Jack said, "when you have everything hanging out where you can see it it's hard not to look. Right Eric? Tomorrow when you go fishing, you catch some too and take them to the Indian village and show Eric your smoker."

Jack called Terry and asked her to meet them at the restaurant for supper.

She said, "Don't you want to come home first and clean up? You have been pouring concrete today, haven't you?"

"We changed at the cabin. We don't look too bad. And we're hungry."

"O.K. I'll meet you there, Bye."

In the morning, Minnow picked up Jack and Eric wearing long pants and a long-sleeved shirt and a jacket.

Eric said, "if you are trying to hide that fine body of yours, I don't know what I said to make you mad, but I'm sorry."

Jack said, "she's going to see her dad today and he doesn't like her to show off her fine body. She's just being safe.

She said, "sometimes I think he doesn't ever want me to get married. He always wants me to dress like an old maid. But thank you for the compliment."

Jack said, "drop me off at the Terry Beth. I need some stuff off of there to work today. While we're there grab a big line to fish with, and that big sack of potatoes to take with you."

Eric spent the time on the ride watching the scenery. He was from Washington and the scenery is good there too, but this is better. The way the evergreen forest comes right down to the rocky beaches and the clear water curling onto the rocks. It's amazing.

At the Terry Beth Jack climbed aboard and got the things he needed and got into the skiff and rowed ashore. Minnow got what she wanted and handed them down to Eric and then they took off to go fishing.

When she had the Minnie anchored over the reef, she mounted a pole on the side with a crank handle on one side and a rubber coated wheel on the other. When Eric started getting his pole ready, she stopped him.

She said, "we're not using a pole today. We're using a hand line."

She unrolled a heavy leader with a weight and a bunch of hooks with hoochies on them and handed it to Eric.

She said, "cast that out and when the weight hits bottom, Jerk it up and down a few times."

After a few jerks the line started fighting him.

Minnow said, "here wrap it around this wheel."

She started turning the crank and Eric pulled in the line as it came off the wheel. When the fish were up to the boat, she took the line and Eric started gaffing the fish and throwing them into the boat.

She replaced a hoochie that was missing and handed the line back to Eric. Who said, "you let me fish with a pole when you knew about this all the time?"

She said, "yes but you wouldn't have had all the fun fighting the fish if I had done this to start with. Besides, we need a bunch of fish today we help to feed the whole village. Some of the people can't fish anymore."

He cast the line out and they did it again. After another cast, they had a dozen fish and Minnow pulled the anchor and they headed out.

CHAPTER 8

When they rounded the end of the Island, they hit the Pacific swell which made the boat dance until they turned North in behind another Island.

When they came in sight of the village Eric asked, "which house is yours?"

She said, "the big one in the middle is my dad's. I stay there when I'm here."

She ran the boat up onto the beach and climbed out over the bow with a long line to tie it up with.

People came from the houses, mostly women and children. She waited on the beach until her father showed up. She hugged him and walked down to the boat with him. When they got to the boat she climbed in and started handing the fish to the women. Her father just stood and stared at Eric. When all the fish and the potatoes were handed out, she introduced her dad to Eric.

He said, "who he?"

She said, "he's Captain Jack's son, so be nice."

He just turned and walked away.

She went and untied the line and climbed back

into the boat and started the engine and revved it and backed off the beach and headed back the way they had come.

Eric said, "I thought we were going to spend a little time there."

"Not with the old man in a pissey mood. He would just cause trouble. Do you want to go catch some fish with your pole now?"

"No let's go find a restaurant where I can get a hamburger. I'm getting tired of fish."

"Getting tired of my cooking, huh? Or is it just me?"

"I'm not tired of either one. I like you a lot. But I need a change in diet. Maybe some pizza."

"There is a good pizza place in Wrangle. Call your dad on the radio and ask him if he wants to go for lunch with his friend Dan."

Jack told them to pick him up at the Terry Beth and rowed out in the skiff and was waiting when they arrived.

Jack said, "you didn't stay long at the village. What no fish?"

Minnow said, "we had plenty of fish. The old man was not friendly."

Eric said, "while we unloaded, he just stared at me like I was there to steel something."

"He was probably worried about you steeling his

daughter. Did he talk to her in Indian?"

"Yes, he said something to her, and she answered him. But it wasn't a very long speech." Eric looked at Minnow and asked, "what did he say?"

"None of your business."

"Ah, come on." Jack said. You can tell us. If you don't, we'll start guessing and that can be embarrassing."

She didn't answer for a minute, and then in a small voice said, "he wanted to know if I was going to run off with Eric."

Jack said, "well, what did you say?"

"That I hadn't been asked. But I would if he asked me."

Things were quiet for a few minutes, then Jack said with a big grin on his face, "I had better call Dan and see if he can meet us for lunch."

It was about a forty-five-minute ride to Wrangell, so Jack scooted to the back bench to call Dan. While they were talking, Eric looked at Minnow and said, "you know I'm old enough to be your dad?"

"I don't care, I have been in love with you since we met. I think it is just a vacation friendship to you, But I hoped it would develop into more. I won't say anything to your dad. He will tease me enough as it is."

Eric said, "I need to know something about you. Are you a Christian?"

"I don't know. I believe in God, but I don't know a lot about being a Christian. Is it important?"

"Yes, we are not to marry non-Christians. All that you must do is believe that Jesus is God and that you are a sinner and that he died for your sins. It is a simple thing because if it were not simple some people would not be able to do it. Just pray this prayer with me, dear God, please forgive my sins and let me be with you when I die."

She prayed the prayer and added, "but don't hurry about the dying part I want to live a while yet."

Eric said, "now that you're a Christian, Will you marry me?"

"Yes, I would love to be your wife. Aren't you going to kiss me?"

She let go of the wheel and fell into his arms and the boat started to turn. Jack rushed forward and leaned over them and grabbed the wheel and straitened them out. He said, "scoot over, I'll drive." He had to; the lips seemed to be locked together with super glue.

While eating lunch Jack asked, "what was all that kissing about?"

Minnow said, "Eric asked me to marry him. And I said yes."

"So, you come up here to fish. Then you steal my first mate."

"Yea, how about loaning me some money to buy her a ring."

Dan said, "not only your first mate but your money too. That's funny."

After eating Dan shows them to a jewelry store.

While they are looking at rings, Eric is looking at diamonds, but Minnow says, "I am not fancy enough for a diamond. How about a simple band with a small red stone?"

Eric said, "you are fancy enough for me. What have you got against diamonds?"

"I would be uncomfortable with an expensive ring. I would be afraid to wear it. I might lose it."

"Well pick out something you would like. But make it nice looking. I don't want anyone saying my dad is cheap."

She got a nice ring with a couple of diamonds on the sides and a ruby for the mane stone. She made Eric get a band for him too.

Jack wrote a check on his new account. The store called the bank to check if it was good. Terry called Jack and asked what he was writing big checks for? He said, "to buy a couple of wedding rings."

"For whom?"

"For my son and my first mate. Eric has to go home in a few days, so we need to have a wedding in the next couple of days. Start planning. But no pressure." She hung up on him.

Minnow said there was a dress shop in Petersburg. So they said goodbye to Dan and took off for

Petersburg. This time Jack drove.

When they got to Petersburg Jack gave Minnow three hundred dollars to buy a dress. She spoke. "I will just get a plain white dress that I can wear on the plane. Since I don't have any nice dresses, it will do double duty. Thanks, Jack, for everything." Then she turned and walked into the store.

Jack said, "come on Eric let's go to the courthouse and see about getting a marriage license."

When they got back to the boat to wait for minnow, Eric said, "did you get that toilet put in on the Terry Beth. I think we will spend our honeymoon there, before we get married since I have to get to work as soon as I get home."

"Yea, but when we get home grab a couple of the big water cans and fill them up to fill the tank on the boat with. Or the toilet won't work."

When they were ready to shove off with the water cans. Jack said, "don't pick me up tomorrow. You just enjoy yourselves. There should be plenty of food on board. I'll call you on the radio if I want something."

When Terry walked in, he knew he was going to get yelled at.

She said, "a wedding in two days how is you going to manage that?"

"We're going to have to. Eric has to get back to his Job. I will call Susan and Maggy, between the two of them they will make it work out." He called Susan.

He said, "Susan I have another problem for you to take care of for me."

"What now, you always have a problem. You are a problem."

"My son and your cousin want to get married and leave in three days. Can you manage it?"

"Me? I knew she wanted to marry him, but I didn't think it would happen. Well, we need a place, and some bride's maids and dresses for them, and a preacher. I'll call Maggy."

"I can do the preaching. And I thought of a couple of places. The terry Beth and our back yard. I have the license. You and Maggy take care of the girl stuff. I'll pay for everything."

"You go open an account at the dress shop I'll get her two sisters as Brides Maids and send them to get dresses. I'll get back to you. Bye."

Jack went to the dress shop and open an account the next morning. Then went to the restaurant and talked to them about catering. About noon the pastor of the Baptist church called and said, "We would be glad to have your son's wedding here and the reception in the basement. Maggy called. She gets things done. In Alaska you have to have a state license to marry people, but I would be glad to help." His name was Bob Witcombe. A real nice guy.

Susan called. She said, "O.K. everything is set up for Saturday. What about a wedding dress?"

"She bought one. She said that she wanted a plain white dress so she could wear it on the plane. I hope her whole boobs don't hang out. You know how she is."

"Yea, good luck there. Well, I think we covered it. If you think of anything else call me."

Jack went to the dress shop and since they knew Minnow's size, he bought her a few nice dresses to take with her. And went to the store and got her a big suitcase and went back and packed everything in it. Later he went to Susan's, and she packed Minnow's other clothes and things into the suitcase and Jack took it to the hotel and got a room for them. He called them on the radio and said, "Your wedding is set up for noon on Saturday. I got a room for you at the hotel and packed your bags and took them there. Dan and Carol are coming up. Dan will be your best man. I rented tuxes for us, and Minnow's sisters will be Brides Maids. I bought them dresses, so everything is set. If you say you are calling it off, I will shoot both of you."

Minnow comes on the radio and says, "we are not calling it off. Don't tell me you did all of this yourself?"

"I called Susan and Maggy. But I did a lot. I even picked you out some clothes to take with you. You might want to come stays at the hotel so that you can get cleaned up for the wedding. You must be getting pretty ripe by now."

"We are getting short of water. Where is it being held?"

"At the Baptist church. The reception too. Hope you like the cake."

"We'll leave now. And thanks a lot Jack."

Saturday morning came right on time. Dan and Carol came on the ferry Friday and stayed at Jack and Terry's. Susan called and said, "Maggy and I are going down to the church early to make sure everything is set up right. Did you get Eric his tux?"

"Yes, they are getting ready at the hotel. Terry gave her a big coat to wear so nobody sees her dress until the wedding. Are you taking care of the Brides Maids?"

"Yes, and we took care of the flowers and a photographer too. Don't worry we'll send you a bill.

"You know you should start a new business, weddings in two days. I think you could do good."

"We'll see you later, Jack."

Rev. Bob did a good service, saying what the Bible says about wives submitting to their husbands and Husbands loving their wives as Christ loved the church and died for it. Minnow's dress was modest enough. It showed plenty of cleavage, but not too much. There was no booze at the reception, come on it was a Baptist church. The food was good, and the church was full. I think everyone in town came. Even Minnow's Dad. Jack walked her down the aisle. She wanted it that way. The Brides Maids were just as pretty as Minnow and Eric told Jack that he would talk his son into coming up for a fishing trip too if one of them was the guide.

In the morning, Jack and Terry and Eric and minnow got into the speed boat and headed for Juneau and the airport for a flight home. Dan and Carrol and Minnow's two sisters and Susan and Maggy were all at the dock to see them off. It's a hundred and twenty-five miles to Juneau so they had to leave early. That's about a four-hour trip even in a fast boat. Because of the noise of the motor there was almost no talk between the front seat and the back, but Terry asked Jack, "Is she on birth control?"

"I don't know, but I doubt it."

"Maybe we will have more grandkids."

"Eric thinks that when Ryan sees the pictures of the fish, he caught that he would want to come fishing too."

"So, we may end up with great grandchildren?"

"I know, you are too young to have great grandchildren."

They passed a lot of traffic going north. A lot of tugboats, some pushing barges, some pulling strings of log rafts. A couple of ferries, fishing boats. And pleasure boats. There was a small plane service to Juneau, but Jack and Terry wanted to see them off. Besides Juneau has a Walmart.

When they tied up at a public dock in Juneau everybody needed a bathroom break. Jack offered the girls a bucket, but they decided they could wait. Jack went to find a taxi, while Eric unloaded the bags, and the girls went potty.

Jack came back and said, "we have to walk up town to catch a cab. Since we have time let's look around the shopping area for a little while. We could visit the Red Dog Saloon."

Minnow said, "not me. I don't go into saloons."

Jack said, "have you been run out of that one too?"

"I have never been there before, jerk."

"That is not showing respect for your elders."

"Elders that don't deserve respect, don't get any."

Eric said, "I thought you two liked each other."

Terry said, "That goes on all the time. I'm surprised she hasn't tried to beat him up. She's a real scrapper."

They found the Red Dog Saloon, and all had an Alaska ale. The bar tender checked Minnow's I.D. It was an I.D. card only.

Eric said, "what no driver's license?"

She said, "there are no roads and no car so, no license, no need. Besides we go everywhere by boat."

"Well, I guess I will have to buy you a car and teach you to drive."

They took a cab to the Airport, and everybody hugged everybody goodbye, and Jack gave Minnow three hundred dollars to buy clothes with. He told her to ask Haley to help her.

After the plane took off, they went to Walmart and loaded up with things that the store in Petersburg didn't carry and took a cab back to the dock. Jack paid the cabby and loaded up all the purchases into the boat and covered them with a tarp for it was raining.

Terry got in and said, "I 'm glad you had a top put on this boat. It would have been a miserable ride home without it."

The ride home didn't seem so long because they didn't need to hurry. They saw a pod of killer whales that were going north and slowed to watch them.

It was a time to enjoy each other's company and to watch the scenery.

When they tied up to the dock Jack said, "I'll run up and open the house and start the fire while you get the packages carried up."

She said, "good luck, you know I think Minnow was right, you are a jerk."

They both carried packages. But he did start the fire.

In the morning Jack was at the chandler shop when it opened.

When Susan came in, he said, "as you know, my son stole my help. I need another do either of the sisters want a job?"

"They both do, do you want both?"

"If they are as good at working as Minnow, I can use them."

"Oh yea, I found a backhoe for you. It's kind of small, but if you want to see it it's in Kake."

"Good, I want to take my truck over there today anyway, but I will need one of the girls to go with me and the other one to come over in the boat. How soon can you get them here?"

"They are at my house; they can be there in a few minutes."

"Give them a call then. You know I didn't catch their names at the wedding Saturday, what are they?"

"They are Indian names that I can't even pronounce, you call them whatever you want."

The girls showed up in a little while dressed for work.

Jack asked, "I didn't catch your names at the wedding, what are they?"

The older one said her name. It sounded like Microfilm. So, jack asked,

"Can I call you Mickey?" She nodded.

The other one was harder. Jack asked, "can I call you Sue? It sounded like you have a Sue in there somewhere." She nodded too. Not too talkative.

Jack thanked Susan and the two girls, and he walked down to the boat.

They went around to the fuel dock and gassed up. He showed them how much oil to mix in the gas. He asked, "do you know where the cabin is?"

They both shook their heads, he explained how to get there and asked,

"Which one wants to go over on the ferry with me and who wants to take the boat over? Better question, who knows how to drive?" Mickey said that she knew how but didn't have a license.

He said, "O.K. It looks like Sue is taking the boat. Take me home Sue."

Since all these kids grew up with boats, he wasn't worried.

He said, "You don't need to get to the cabin right away. We won't get there until one or so. take the boat and meet us at the lumber company dock."

They went up to the house and picked up his truck. When they arrived at the Lumber company Sue was there. When they went into the store Jack introduced the girls to Deke and told him they would be picking up things for him. Deke said, "what happened to Minnow?"

Jack said, "she ran off with my son. These are her sisters."

He said, "I know I was at the wedding. They sure looked great all dressed up. What are you after today?"

"Wiring. By the way did you get a price on that solar roofing?"

"Yea, boy that stuff is spendy. Here is a paper on it."

"I'll figure what I need and let you know. Today, wiring and tools for these girls.

They went to the café for lunch. By the time they finished it was time to get the truck on the ferry. When they arrived at Kake they drove the truck off the ferry and asked directions to where to see the backhoe.

When they saw it Mickey said, "It looks like a riding mower with a toy back hoe on the back."

Jack talked to the owner and tried it out. It would do. He bought it.

He told Mickey to follow him in the truck and headed for the cabin.

He didn't want to drive across the bridge yet, so they parked on the other side and walked over. First, they uncovered the cement. It looked good. He took the hose still running into the creek and watered it down and put the hose back into the creek.

Mickey asked, "where does the water come from?"

"From the creek up the hill. Now that we have a backhoe, we will run it underground to the house. Then we can put in a toilet and get rid of the outhouse. Let's carry in the wire, it looks like it's going to rain.

They worked until Sue showed up and then locked up and went home.

When they were tied up at the dock bye his house, Jack said, "come early and I'll buy you breakfast. We are going to have to work hard to make up for Minnow being lazy and doing nothing but fishing the last two weeks."

They knew the true story and just laughed and

walked away.

The next morning, they were at the boat when Jack got there.

After eating they got into the boat and with Sue driving headed to the cabin. When they arrived, he told Sue to run it up on the sand. The tide was almost all the way out, so he threw a small anchor off the stern and tied it off. Then climbed out over the bow with a long line to tie off the bow.

He unlocked and had the girls take shovels and climb down under the house to level the dirt off to make a room down there. He went to work on the wiring. By noon the girls were done in the basement. They had brought their lunches, so they ate. Jack kept working. He didn't eat lunch. It rained the next two days, so they worked on the wiring and finished the plumbing that had been mostly done when he bought the place.

When the weather cleared up, he got the backhoe across the bridge and put in a septic system and a water line to the house from far enough up the hill that they would have good water pressure in the house.

Jack was getting tired of the outhouse and since they now had water and a septic system, he wanted a toilet. There was a hardware store in Kake that carried some lumber. But not enough. So, they took the Terry Beth to Petersburg and loaded up with insulation and drywall and drywall mud, and a toilet and a sink and hard wood for the floor, and paint.

They used the boom to load everything onto the beach. Then drove the truck down there and in three trips, hauled it all up to the house and stacked it inside. In a few days they dry walled, painted, laid the floor, hooked up the sink and toilet. And when they came the next day they brought a door, the girls insisted. They then went to work on the rest of the house.

The girls were good workers and learned fast.

Jack complimented them on their taping and finishing work.

Jack bought a cement mixer in Kake and bags of cement. He wanted to pour a slab in the basement before he put in the wood stove but knew that he couldn't get a cement truck down on that side of the house.

While the girls finished the dry wall work, he took the backhoe and hauled sand from the beach to the house to mix cement with. Then he cut a hole in the wall for a window that he could shovel sand through.

It took them a whole day to pour the slab, with Sue running the mixer, Mickey carrying the buckets of cement through the window and Jack working the cement. They were a tired crew at the end of the day.

The next day they hauled the materials for the chimney from Kake and built that. He wanted to get the wood stove hooked up. It was almost fall. He wanted to make sure he had heat when it got cold. He had the girls insulate and drywall the basement wall next to the chimney while he built the stairs into the basement. The next day they picked up the wood stove from the lumber company in Petersburg and hauled it over in the Minny. Sue pulled the boat next to the beach and they put a strap around the stove and lifted it out of the boat with the front-end loader of the backhoe and hauled it to the house and put it in through the window. Jack built a hearth and the wall protection out of stone that the girls hauled from the beach with the backhoe. From the lumber company the next day, they brought a widow for the basement and the pipes to hook up the stove.

Jack bought the materials in Kake to build a woodshed. When it was done, he took his chain saw and cut up downed timber between his house and Kake. He didn't know who owned the land, but he thought he was doing them a favor, cleaning up the dead timber.

Anyway, nobody said anything. There was a lot of it.

They took four truckloads of ten- and twelve-foot logs.

Then he cut them into rounds and the girls split and stacked the pieces in the woodshed. One girl ran the splitter and the other stacked. When the shed was full Jack figured he had six cords. They had plenty of wood to keep the place warm while they were working on it, but when winter came they would have to drain the water system to save it from freezing.

They would be done before the real cold weather

came.

Now they were doing the finish work so it would only be a couple of weeks. While the girls did the finish work, Jack built the garage. When all was done Jack called Maggy and asked her if she wanted to list it. She came right over. She looked the house over and said, "Jack it looks great. You should list it for ninety thousand. It's worth all of that."

"Whatever you say, Maggy, you're the expert. Does this cove freeze over in the winter?"

"The cove probably does because of the creek running into it. But the bay doesn't." She hung a lock box on the door and put up some for-sale signs and said goodbye and left. Jack and Mickey pulled in the anchors on the Terry Beth and headed for home with Sue driving the Minny.

The next day they went back for the truck and tractor. They got the tractor on the back of the truck, but Jack told Mickey to ride along in case the ferry didn't like it and they would need two drivers. Sue took the Minney home.

Three weeks later Jack got an offer on the cabin for eighty-five and countered at eighty-seven and it was sold. Jack did the math and said he cleared thirty thousand. He gave the girls a bonus.

Dan called and said, "I hear you sold your cabin. Congrats."

"Yes, it went well. How are you guys doing?"

"We're doing good. Hey, I might have a job for you. There's a guy here that needs a shipment of stuff brought up from Ketchikan. It would be a good load for your big boat. You interested?"

"Sure, now that the cabin is done, we need something to do. Give me his number. And thanks."

Two days later they were on the way to Ketchikan for some freight to haul back to Wrangell. Being five hours each way, they left at six in the morning. That way they would make it back in time to get unloaded before quitting time. As they cruised along, Mickey was at the wheel. Jack was just watching the scenery go bye. He said, I can't believe I will ever get tired of this. It's beautiful, and we're getting paid for it too."

It was an easy trip a crane at the dock in Ketchikan loaded the pallets into the hold and when they got to Wrangell the customer had a boom truck there to unload them. Jack had left notices in Ketchikan at the port captain's office, the dock office and with the crane operator. Maybe they would get some calls. The notice read, Captain Jack and the Terry Beth are available to haul freight around the Islands for a very reasonable fee. Call ----------

Dan came to the dock while they were unloading and asked them to have dinner with him and Carol.

So, they left the boat tied to the dock and went and had dinner with Dan and Carol. They still made it home before dark.

While Jack was seeing Eric and Minnow off in Juneau,

he had left a couple of his notices there too. He got a call asking for a price to haul a load to Sitka. He gave them a price and they said, "You got the job when can you do it?" He said, "I can be there about noon. Will that do?"

"Yes, we'll have a crane to load you, standing by." He called the girls.

Mickey said, "The Indians have three totem poles to take to Juneau. If you take them, we will work for free on this trip."

He said, "You mean, If I haul them for free you will work for free?"

"We will also bring the food."

"Are you as good at cooking as Minnow?"

"We all learned at the same time, by the same woman."

"O.K. get over here now because we need to pick up those poles now, so we can leave by four in the morning."

It took seven hours to get to Juneau. Jack took a two-hour nap and so did Mickey. They took the narrow channel to the northeast of Admiralty Island. Jack was surprised at all the traffic. The people for the Totem poles were ready for them when they arrived. So, there was no hold up.

When they tied up at the cargo wharf the crane loaded them right away while Jack collected for hauling the load to Sitka.

They were told that fuel was cheaper in Juneau, so they refueled there before heading out. Sue went down below and went to sleep. It was going to be a long day. There is a lot of time to think while you are at the wheel of a slow-moving boat. He was thinking that he really liked this job, traveling through these beautiful Islands and getting paid for it too. And with two pretty girls along to flirt with. He couldn't think of a better life.

To pass the time Mickey was telling him about her life. She said that staying at Susan's was great. Her and Sue had single beds in one room. But she loved the hot shower after a day's work. At the Indian village the whole family lived in a one room cabin with an outhouse. No hot shower. The hot shower alone was worth the rent they paid Susan.

Jack said, "Sorry, no hot shower on the boat."

She said, "at least you have a toilet and not a bucket to poop in. And the bunks are comfortable. I knew the boat before you got it, they didn't have it so nice. You have better equipment and radios. I think we could navigate through thick fog with what we have. I really like this old boat. I hope you keep me working for you."

"It all depends on if you are as good a cook as Minnow."

She did a real good job on dinner that night.

They hit the open sea just before getting into Sitka. It got a little rough but not bad. Sue came up from below saying, "you guys couldn't let me sleep in piece for a while without trying to tip the boat over could you."

Mickey said, "We didn't want you to miss dinner. We have sour dough biscuits and fish stew. Made from some of the fish that our brother-in-law Eric caught."

"I don't know, I think I like sleep better."

Jack called the number that they had given him. The man answering told him where to tie up. They had a crane there to unload him. The dock hand said there was a skiff they could use if they wanted to anchor out and go ashore. Sue went and found the skiff and rowed out and they all changed clothes and rowed ashore to see the town. Jack took some flyers to leave here and there. Maybe they could pick up a load to take home. They stopped in a couple of bars just to look around. Mickey was asked to dance by a young fellow who was the size of Eric. She danced with him and Jack and Sue danced to a couple of songs. They were having a good time. Then a guy came over and tried to cut in with Sue. She said no thanks and he grabbed her and said, "you're going to dance with me and like it." Jack hit him. He went down and two more guys came charging in. Things were getting a little crazy when the guy dancing with Mickey showed up. He took out one of two Jack was having a sporting event with, and Jack knocked out the other. Jack thought it a good time to leave before the cops showed up. Outside they thanked the big guy whose name was Dave Whitehead and headed for the boat. Dave asked for Mickey's phone number. She gave him Jack's and said, "We have a boat that we haul freight with and that's our only number. Or you can call us on the radio. It's the Terry Beth." He walked them down to the bay and said he would call them in the morning. He did too. Mickey rowed to the dock and picked him up to come have breakfast on the boat. Sue cooked some smoked fish on the barbe and served it with some special sauce. On the stove in the cabin, she made pancakes and coffee. Dave had a lot of questions about hauling freight around the Islands. He said, "I envy you Jack, having two beautiful girls as a crew to spend a lot of time with. And the pleasure of cruising the Islands and getting paid for it too."

"Do you know of any business for us?"

"There is a family moving to Wrangell that have been looking for a way to move their furniture. We could give them a call and see what happens."

Jack handed his phone to Dave and using the 411 operator he got the number and called and told the people that he had a way to transport their furniture, were they still looking? They said yes, so he handed the phone back to Jack and he made a deal with them. They would get all of their stuff down to the dock and he and his crew would get it loaded aboard the boat.

Jack signaled to Mickey to go into the cabin to talk and excused himself and went in. Mickey came in a minute later. He said, "do you want to take Dave along to Wrangell? We could get him a ferry ticket home. He would be a help loading."

"I'm not in love with him Jack but it might be fun. I'll ask him."

She went out on the deck and said, "When we go to load that furniture would you like to come along and watch? You could see how two girls and an old man do it."

He said, "I would love to. Those people are friends of mine I will even be glad to help." When Jack got the call that the furniture was on the dock, He told Mickey to row the skiff back to where she got it and walk to the dock. Dave wanted to go along, so they went. Sue got the anchor up and they moved to the loading dock. Jack handed pallets up to Sue to load the furniture on so they could use the boom to swing the loaded pallets on board.

By the time Mickey and Dave got there they had one pallet loaded and tied down and were working on the second. Then the people who owned the stuff showed up with more to load. Dave introduced them as Tom Ellis and his wife Karen. They had two boys, Tom Jr. 10 and Jim 8. The boys were all excited about the boat and everything else. With everybody helping, in an hour the pallets were all loaded and swung aboard and tied down. Jack had them put a big tarp over it all in case of rain. Mickey whispered to Jack, "they are short of money, how about asking them if they would like to ride with us. Instead of waiting for the ferry."

"I'm not licensed to haul passengers."

"Sign them on as crew. The boys would love it."

"You ask them. And tell them that the boys will have to wear life jackets all the time."

They were all very thankful. Dave asked if he could go too. To help get their stuff to the house they rented. Jack agreed. He started the motor, Mickey made smoked fish sandwiches, and Sue got the lines in and then started a big pot of fish stew and sour dough biscuits to feed everybody at dinner time. The shortest trip was out to sea and around the Islands. But even that was seven hours at best. As he pulled out around the harbor mouth, he saw that the sea was calm enough. So, no worries, mate as the Aussies say.

CHAPTER 9

The boys were having a ball checking everything out. They each took a turn at the wheel with Jack standing by.

Just before they reached the south end of the Island, Dave came in.

He said, "there is a big wave coming up from the rear. You better look."

Sue took the wheel. He went out and looked and ran back in and took the wheel and turned the boat as fast as she would go around. He just made it in time to head into the swell. It probably would have capsized them if it caught them from the rear. Sue and Karen saved the pots from falling off the stove. Though Sue did get burned some on her arms. She was soon cooling them under cold water. Jack slowed the motor but kept the boat heading NNW there were always more big waves after an earthquake. The first was the biggest but until he got a look at them, he kept his course. Mickey came in and said, "we shipped some water, but I think the tarp kept the cargo dry." Tom said, "don't worry about it, it's just stuff as long as everyone is O.K. it's all good." Karen said, "Sue got burned, do you have something to put on it?"

"In the medicine cabinet there's burn spray." Jack said.

The boys came in wet to the knees, Jim said, "we were at the back end when that big wave splashed over the side and caught us. Mickey showed us how to work the pumps, so we got to help pump the water out. It was neat."

Karen looked worried, but Tom Sr. laughed and said, "the boys will remember this trip for a long time. I'm glad that you made them wear life jackets."

Jack said, "stand by for the next wave, here she comes." It was not so big, and the boat took it without shipping any water. Jack watched as the wave swept along the shore of the Island far up into the timber and picking up all the driftwood along the beach that the first wave missed. There would be a lot of drift logs in the water now and they would have to keep a close watch. After the next wave, which was smaller than the last, He turned around and headed SSE. He told Mickey to put on a life jacket and to climb up on the bow and watch for drift logs. They had to go a little slower to dodge the debris in the water, but after five hours they rounded the second Island and headed east for Wrangell. Jack called Dan and said, "Dan this is Jack, Is Wrangell still on the map?"

"Yea, we had some warning, so we got most of the boats away from shore and moved most everything movable inland. How did you guys make out?"

"Nothing too serious, but we could use some help. We have a family and their furniture aboard and they are moving there, and we could use a truck to move their stuff to the house they rented. And if I give you the address maybe you could check and see if it is still standing."

"No problem, Jack gives me the address and I'll call you back. How long before we see your sorry self?"

"About two hours. If these waves don't quit coming, we may have to wait to land this stuff until morning."

"Yea, the docks took a beating, but we should be able to tell by the time you get here. I'll get back to you."

They sat up lawn chairs and a folding table on the deck and Jack prayed a prayer of thanks for the food and for saving their lives and they ate the fish stew and drank root beer.

Karen said, "this is the best stew I've ever tasted. Do you pay these girls extra for their cooking?"

"I keep two of them on when I only need one."

Tom said, "is everyone on the crew Christians?"

"No, the girls are some heathen Indian religion. But I have orders from their sister to work on them. But the old insurance spiel doesn't work, because they don't own anything but the clothes on their backs."

"What is the insurance spiel?"

"You know, if you own a car, you have car insurance. If you have a house, you have fire insurance.

Well, being a Christian is a type of fire insurance on your soul."

Mickey said, "He is always coming up with weird stuff. He did get our sister converted by saying she couldn't marry his son without being saved. I think he plans to try that on us when his grandsons come up to go fishing."

Jack said, "well, being a Christian works for me, look it saved all of us from a Tsunami. And a couple of times a little voice kept me from getting bit by poisonous snakes. Don't knock it."

Mickey said, "are your grandsons as big as your son?"

"No, they are little guys my size."

Tom said, "If you are a little guy, I'm littler. I'm five ten. You must be six one. By the way we're Christians too."

Jack said "good, I won't have to spend a lot of time preaching at you then."

An hour later Dan called back. He said, "Well, your people lucked out. The house is high enough that the water didn't get to it. And I will have a truck at the city dock when you get here. Will you need help unloading?"

"No, we have plenty of help. You will like these people. They will make good neighbors for you. Is the house near yours?"

"Just a couple of blocks away. Carol and I will be

glad to meet them. I borrowed the boom truck so we can unload right onto it. And Carol will be there with the car to haul people."

"Good, thanks a lot Dan. See you soon."

"Get the fenders out Mickey, I don't want to bang up against the dock if another wave hits us while we're tied up there." Dave and Tom helped Mickey get the tarp off the cargo and Dan dropped the ball down and Jack hooked it up and tom climbed up and unhooked the straps. And so, the pallets were all loaded onto the truck quickly and tied down.

Leaving Sue with the boat, they all rode with Dan and Carol to the rented house and unloaded the truck and moved everything in. Karen directed traffic. And everything got set up to her liking. Carol drove Jack and Dave and Mickey back to the boat. Jack handed her a hundred bucks and said, "If that isn't enough send me a bill. I really appreciate all your help. I hope you become good friends with Tom and Karen, they are nice folks.

"You know Dan won't want the money."

"Don't tell him I know you can use it. Besides, my job would be a lot harder if you two didn't help me with things like this. Thanks again."

It would be late when they got there, but they decided to go on home for the night. It was almost midnight when they tied up to Jack's dock. They put the fenders out in case of more waves. Dave decided to sleep on the boat. The rest went home. As soon as

Jack got home, he went in and took a shower. When he came out Terry said, "I was worried about you did the tsunami catch you?"

"Yea, but we saw it coming and turned into it. We didn't lose anybody or anything, so we were fortunate."

"Was it a good trip?"

"Yea, we had to haul totem poles for the Indians for free to Juneau, but we would have been running empty if we didn't do it. We did good from Juneau to Sitka and from Sitka to Wrangell. So, we made some friends and a profit. We brought a family and their goods to Wrangell. Dan and Carol helped on that end."

When Jack got up in the morning, he went down to check on Dave, but Mickey was already there making him breakfast. She made some for Jack too. Jack told Dave "The girls had wanted him to Haul some totem poles for their village for free. We did it but I told them that in payment they would have to go to church with me and today is Sunday. Would you like to go too?"

"Sure, but I will need to clean up first."

Jack took him home and he showered and shaved, and Jack gave him some clean clothes and told him that he could catch a ferry right after church. And he would pay for it for helping.

Mickey and Sue in pretty dresses and Dave cleaned up and Jack and Terry all went to the little

Baptist Church and were greeted by Rev. Bob.

When church was over, they all walked Dave down to the ferry landing and Jack bought him a ticket to Sitka. He asked Dave if he needed money.

Dave said, "No, I'm O.K. but thanks and thank you for the adventure. I won't forget that trip for a while. You guys have an exciting life."

Jack said, "It was great having you along and the next trip to Sitka we'll give you a call. We can do lunch or something. Or maybe drag you along on another trip." Dave hugged the girls and went down the landing to the ferry and waved goodbye.

As they walked home Terry asked Mickey, "do you like that guy?"

"Yes, but he's a logger and like miners they only work half the year and are always broke. If you marry one you end up supporting them."

Jack said, "she is waiting for the grandsons. She thinks they will be as good-looking as Eric and will take her away from here like Minnow.

Terry said, "Cody is even better looking than Eric. Not as tall but built like him. But Ryan is handsome too."

Mickey asked, "who is older"

"Cody is twenty-three and just out of the marines. Ryan is twenty-one but has a good job and owns his own home. They are both good catches. And as pretty as you two are you will catch them if you try."

"Thank you, Terry, for saying we're pretty. Will it matter that we're Indians?"

"Not a bit, I think that you three girls are the most beautiful women I've ever seen. Jack would be after you too, even at his age if I didn't threaten to shoot him if he did."

Jack said, "she would too. We don't have any loads scheduled for a couple of days, and I need to get some writing done, so take some time off."

"How about if we anchor the Terry Beth out and take the Minny and see our folks?"

"Yea sure, if you need some money come to the house. Pay day is tomorrow anyway."

"No, if we have money dad will take it from us. We will wait until tomorrow. Besides, we have to have money to pay Susan for our room and board. If dad takes our money we might get kicked out at Susan's."

CHAPTER 10

J ack worked on his book for a few days. Terry called the grandsons and told them they needed to come fishing before winter hit. Cody called back and said, "I will come if grandpa buys me a ticket. I haven't gone to work yet and I'm about broke."

Terry said, "you won't need any money. You can stay with us and use our boat and one of the girls will show you where to fish. And how to smoke them and even how to get them shipped home. I'll get you a ticket on the way."

She got him a flight to Juneau and a float plane flight to Petersburg.

He landed three days later at the ferry landing. Mickey and Sue met him with the Minney. They took him to Jack's house in the boat and walked with him to show him the way. It was almost dinner time, so they went in and got dinner ready while Jack and Terry and Cody got caught up on things.

Cody asked, "do the girls always cook for you?"

Terry said, "they are so much better cooks than me that I always ask them to cook for us when they are in town."

"Are they out of town a lot?"

"They work for Jack on the big boat hauling freight around the Islands. They are gone a lot."

"I can see why grandpa has them working for him. They are very pretty. I didn't believe Eric when he said they were as pretty as Minnow. But boy was I wrong. They are beautiful. Do they live here?"

"No, they stay with a cousin three blocks away."

They are not only pretty, but they are also quiet and that is strange for a woman.

They are so much alike; you would think they are twins."

"Well, only fall in love with one. You need to save one for Ryan."

After dinner Cody asked if He could walk the girl's home. On the way he said, "which one of you is the best cook? That was the best fish dinner I've ever eaten."

Sue said, "Jack says that Mickey is better, but I did the cooking tonight.

We all learned from the same woman at the same time, so we are probably about the same. Did you eat any of Minnow's cooking at home?"

"Oh yea, Eric is very proud of her cooking. He invited the whole family over for dinner."

Mickey asked, "how are they doing?"

"They seem very happy; Eric didn't want to go back to work. He just wanted the honeymoon to last longer." They had arrived home. And said goodnight and went in. Cody walked back to his grandpa's house.

In the morning when Cody came in for breakfast, the girls were already there talking with Terry. Jack was eating. Cody sat down and Terry asked him what he would like for breakfast. He saw that Jack was eating pancakes, so he said, "I'll have what he's got. Aren't you ladies eating?"

Mickey said, "we ate earlier. We don't sleep this late. We all have jobs to do."

Cody asked, "Do You have a trip today?"

Mickey said, "Jack and Sue are making a run. I am playing fishing guide. And Terry is running the bank. When you are done eating, we will go find some big ones to match your uncle Erics."

"I think I would like to go on the run. How long will you be gone?"

Jack said, "It's just to Ketchikan and back. We'll be back tonight."

"Can I come too?"

"Yea sure, At the other end we will be loaded with a crane. But at this end we will probably need to unload by hand. We can use the help."

Mickey said, "maybe fishing sounds better now, huh?"

Jack said, "make up your mind we're leaving."

Cody said, "Do I have time to eat?"

Mickey said, "yes, Jack and Sue are going out to bring the boat in, while I make lunches. Everything is on the table so help yourself."

They made a stop at the fuel dock to gas up. Cody asked Mickey, "you just have one outboard for power? How come?"

"That one motor will push the boat faster than our hull speed when we're empty and it's just right when we're fully loaded. We don't need more."

"What do you mean hull speed?"

"Each type of boat has a hull speed. If you try to go faster than that it will broach. That means it turns sideways. The hull speed on this boat is about fifteen knots."

"It must take a long time to get anywhere."

"This trip will take about fourteen hours round trip. Did you have somewhere special that you wanted to go?"

"Why do I get the feeling that you are always laughing at me?"

"It's only because you are not from here. If I ever come to Seattle, I will be out of my element, and you can laugh at me. Just about no one up here has a driver's license. There are almost no roads. We go everywhere by boat. So, we know what the hull speed is. It is kind of funny though. Has Minnow got a driver's license yet?"

"No but that doesn't stop her from driving."

Cody was Impressed with the scenery and the traffic. He went into the wheelhouse and said, "I had no Idea that so much stuff moved by water up here. There are tugboats and small steamers and ferries going in both directions. And all kinds of yachts and fishing boats too."

"There are no roads up here. Everything goes through here. This is the inland waterway. If you keep your eyes open, you will see whales too."

Jack told Mickey to get him a lawn chair and some binoculars and take him up on the roof where he will be able to see more. When he was settled, she got herself a chair and two beers and joined him. She told Cody, "Where we are going in Ketchikan a dock worker threw a full can of beer at a deckhand on one of the boats. It hit him right in the head."

"What happened, was he hurt?"

"No, it was light beer."

"Oh brother, you have been around grandpa too long."

On arrival at Ketchikan, they were loaded right away, but at the office the foreman said, "we have a pallet load for Sitka. Do you want it?"

Jack checked the shipping order. It wouldn't pay a lot, but it would pay enough for expenses. So, they took it too. As soon as they were tied down Jack shoved off. Mickey came in and looked at the paperwork. She said,

"Sitka, you won't make much on that one."

"It gives me something to do. And we will leave you and Cody at home to go fishing. Maybe we will pick up something from there."

Since it looked like rain Jack had the girls put the tarp over everything and strap it down. Along toward dinner time Mickey made smoked fish soup and sour dough biscuits. Cody ate more than his share.

Cody said, "Minnow made soup like that, but yours was better."

Jack said, "It always tastes better at sea. But I like Mickey's better too."

When they reached Petersburg, they swung the three pallets ashore and they were picked up by the hardware store people. They refueled at the fuel dock and Mickey and Cody got off and the Terry Beth headed for Sitka.

Jack decided on the inside passage. It was a little bit farther, but less rough. Sue took first watch and Jack went below to sleep. They pulled into Sitka at five in the morning. There was no one at the dock that early so Jack dropped Sue off to borrow a skiff and went out and dropped anchor to wait.

Sue rowed out in a skiff and came in and made breakfast. At seven the dock foreman showed up. They pulled the anchor and pulled up to the dock and Jack went in to check with the foreman. When he came back he told Sue that they had a cargo for Juneau that they would load as soon as they were unloaded. At Juneau they picked up a load for Yakutat. It was a good size load, so they went out around Glacier Bay Nat'l Park and headed NW up the coast. The sea was calm, so they made the two hundred miles without any trouble. They didn't get anything going back. But in Juneau they picked up a load for Skagway. And one back to Juneau. Then from Juneau to Wrangell.

They had lunch with Dan and Carol and went home. It was almost Thanksgiving and Cody had gone home. Mickey and Terry were waiting on the dock when they pulled in.

Mickey started the Minney and went out to where they were anchoring the Terry Beth to pick them up. When they got to shore Jack said, "well we saw a lot of country and we made some money. We have a bunch of checks to deposit, so we'll be going to the bank tomorrow."

Terry said, "we didn't miss you, we had Cody to keep us entertained."

Jack asked, "Did he propose to Mickey? I see she's still here."

Mickey said, "he said that he didn't even have a job and was staying with his grandma. That the timing was bad. But he said that he liked my cooking."

Terry said, "I think he'll be back. He does need to

get settled in first. He is smart." It's not what Mickey wanted to hear but she knew that it was right.

Jack asked, "did Cody catch plenty of fish and get them all smoked up and shipped and everything?"

Mickey said, "Yea, and you paid for it all."

After thanksgiving, a shipping agent from Ketchikan called and said he had some cargo for Craig and Klawock and Hydaburg. Jack told him they would be there in the morning. And so, it went. They were up and down the Islands for three weeks before they were home again. With three of them though to stand watch it was four hours on and eight hours off. That was better than four on and four offs when there was just the two of them.

Jack decided to stop work until after Christmas. He needed to do some writing. The girls were glad for the break too.

They decided to go see their family for a few days. Since they didn't have phones, they took a radio with them. They were only there two days when Susan called them on the big CB radio at the chandler shop. She said,

"Jack got a call from Ketchikan; they have a load for Sitka that is urgent. At least one of you needs to go." Sue called back, "Roger, but the village has some totems for Ketchikan. So, tell Jack to come pick us up. Over."

"O.K. I'll pass on the message, out."

One of the girls raced back in the Minny to help Jack get the anchor in and get underway.

At the village they pulled up alongside the dock and got the totems aboard with the boom. There were four and as soon as they were loaded, they left for Ketchikan. Jack called the people from the Totem Pole Park and told them to please have a truck there at seven in the morning. He needed to be unloaded by seven thirty.

When the crane operator got there in the morning, the poles were gone, and they got loaded right away. As soon as they were underway, Mickey asked, "what makes this load urgent, anyway?"

"It's hospital supplies and they are late getting here. The dock foreman told them that our boat was faster than the freighter. So, they asked for us. And are paying extra. Even though it's still two weeks until Christmas, we won't try to get a load back."

They made Sitka by four, so they were unloaded right away.

The man from the hospital asked, "Since you are going back to Petersburg, could you drop some supplies at the Indian village near there. We have a nurse stationed there and she needs a few things."

Jack said, "Sure, and no charge these girls are from that village. We'll be glad to help."

It was a small pallet load. Mickey said, "That was

nice of you not to charge them Jack."

Jack said, "Yea, It's good for business. Now next time they need a load hauled. They will think of us first and they pay good."

While they were there, Mickey called Dave and asked if he would like to come to the boat for dinner. He said he was working and couldn't make it, but thanks for the invite. They headed for home.

When they arrived at the village dock it was early morning. When the pallet was swung to the dock Sue said she would stay with it. And that Mickey could pick her up later, whenever.

When the Terry Beth was anchored Mickey dropped Jack at his dock and went to Susan's. Jack went to town. His wife was at work, so he went Christmas shopping and to the bank to make his deposits.

He stopped by the real estate office to say hi to Maggy.

She said, "Are you going to buy or build another cabin this next year?"

"No, I need to get some writing done. And the boat is taking up too much time. I used to run it with one helper. Now I need two, or I don't get enough sleep. The trip before last we ran out of food we were gone so long.

When I get these girls married off, I might sell the boat and retire."

"If you did, we wouldn't call you Captain Jack

anymore. And the name is becoming famous. You have even been written up in the local piracy journal."

Jack started his book on moving to Alaska. He wrote this poem to go with it.

Jack was an old man of seventy-two, who hardly ever had a cold or the flu because of his age he couldn't find work except delivering papers or as a soda jerk. A friend from Alaska said try up there too. If you're healthy they can surely use you. He put his truck on a ferry and rode up on the sea. Now he lives in Alaska and is happy as can be.

Well, it's not too bad. His wife liked it. But he decided not to try writing a book of poetry.

Mickey and Sue came in and said it was snowing. That they needed to do something about the Terry Beth enough snow might sink her.

He called Susan. She said, "There is a guy in Wrangell that can make a tarp for it. You will have to put some tie downs on the outside of the hull, but with the boom for a center pole it would work. Jack went down and made some drawings and took measurements and put the girls to putting on tie downs around the hull and left for Wrangell. The girls were using the skiff. Susan had called ahead so Jack got to see the man right away. He said he would have the tarp ready for a fitting in two days. Jack had lunch with Dan and Carol. She was pregnant and he had a job, and they were happy.

Jack headed for home to shovel snow if he didn't

get lost in the snow.

Two days later they pulled the anchor and headed for Wrangell.

With Sue at the wheel Jack and Mickey shoveled snow. By the time they reached Wrangell, most of it was over the side. The man with the tarp was at the dock when they arrived. Dan came down to help. It took all of them to get that big tarp stretched out along the boom. Then standing on the dock they got one side hooked onto the tie downs. Sue turned the boat around and they hooked on the other side. The man whose name was Barny showed them how to tighten the ropes and it fit tight. Jack paid Barny and they went to lunch at Carol's Café. At Lunch Dan said, "I think if you put a heater under that tarp, it would melt off the rest of the snow and the pumps would get rid of it for you.

"That's a good idea. We have a little Propane heater we can try it on the way home." Mickey said.

After lunch, they said goodbye and crawled through the flap in the back and zipped it up behind them and headed for home. Jack hooked up the little heater in the back and went into the wheelhouse and sat down to some coffee. It was still snowing, but the wipers were keeping it off the windshield. The GPS showed them where they were, but Jack was a little worried about running into another boat. You could Hardly see beyond the bow. They probably would have hit that ferry, but it had on its foghorn, so they got out of the way in time. With just one close call they made it home OK. Jack was surprised how warm it was under the tarp. The rest of the snow was all gone too. Barney said that could tie the tarp up around the boom if they needed to haul freight.

Jack was pretty sure that with just two of them they couldn't do it.

The snow kept falling for five days. He taught Mickey and Sue how to run the backhoe and they made money clearing driveways while Jack kept writing. No more poems though.

The tractor has a roof but no side curtains, so the girls took turns driving. One driving and one thawing out. It was cold work.

Jack had his computer by the wood stove, so he was nice and warm.

The girls were busy from early until late. Jack let them keep the money they made but they had to pay for the fuel. They did good. When it finally quit snowing there was more than four feet on the ground. It took the girls three days of work after it quit before they stopped getting calls.

The snow kind of stopped freight from moving too. So, they didn't get any calls until after Christmas. Another load from Ketchikan to Sitka. They stopped at Wrangell and Dan helped them roll up the tarp and get it tied to the boom. It had worked fine. They called Dave when they reached Sitka and he said that he had some more friends that were moving and needed a lift. It was to the town of Douglas next to Juneau. So, they unloaded the freight and loaded the furniture and went to Douglas. Picked up a load for Yakutat. No load going back but Jack left some flyers. Maybe someday.

They went back to Juneau and picked up a load for Sitka again.

While they were unloading the Hospital called and asked if they would take another small pallet to the Indian village again. They would pay them this time. After dropping off the pallet at the village they went home.

A week later Ketchikan called with another load of freight for the Hospital in Sitka. The dock foreman said Jack's rate was cheaper than the freighter. So, get to work.

A beverage company in Juneau wanted to send a pallet load of booze to Skagway, No return fare. But one from Juneau to Angoon. Since they were close to home they went home. It started to snow again. They managed to get the tarp up by themselves.

Jack went back to writing and the girls to plowing snow.

Cody called, he said, "I have some news. It won't be really important to you, but I got a job as a security guard at a big plant in Seattle. I rented a nice apartment near there and got some furniture from rent to own, So I am all set up to marry Mickey."

"Have you asked her yet?"

"No, she doesn't have a phone. Would you ask

her to call me? It needs to be after six I don't get home till then."

"Sure, let me write that down so I don't forget. What's your number again?"

"Come on Grandpa, this is important."

"Sounds important, if you just got the job, are they going to give you time off to get married?"

"No, but I have four days off in three weeks, maybe Grandma could get it set up for that date."

"You are asking a lot when you haven't even asked the girl yet. Give me the dates. I'll tell Terry but she's getting tired of these last-minute weddings. I suppose I have to pay for it too. And pay for the air fare too."

"Thanks for offering Grandpa, I really appreciate it. Don't forget have Mickey call me please."

Jack called Susan at work and asked her to tell Mickey to come see him when she got in. Susan said sure, what's up?

Jack said, "Cody wants to propose and get married in three weeks."

Susan laughed and said, "Well at least he's giving us three weeks. Are you paying for this one too?"

"You guessed it; I will not run out of Grandkids before you run out of cousins though."

"I have more cousins."

"Well, find me an ugly one, then maybe I can keep one for a crew."

"Sorry Jack, I don't have any ugly ones. I'll send word to Mickey that she's needed. By Jack."

"By and thanks."

Mickey showed up a half hour later. Jack told her to sit down, that they had some serious things to discuss. She took off her coat and sat down.

He said, "Cody called, He wants you to call him. He wants to ask you to marry him. He waited until he had a job and a place to live before he asked you. But there is a problem. You are not a Christian."

She flared up and said, "Did he say that?"

"No, I did. I'm the head of my family and It's my responsibility. The Bible says not to marry an unbeliever. So, I can tell you how to become a Christian."

"We can be married without your permission."

"That's true, is that the way you want it? If so, you had better talk it over with Cody. But I'm sorry that you feel that way. It would make an unhappy marriage. Well, here is Cody's phone number. He said to call after six, that he doesn't get home until then." She left angry at jack.

She went right to see Susan and told her all about it. Susan said,

"Cody probably won't marry you without his grandfather's blessing. So, you had better think over your options. If you want Cody, you had better change your attitude. My husband wouldn't marry me until I became a Christian too. I'm not sorry that I did. The Bible has rules to live by. It's like a owner's manual. He that made us tells us the best way to live. You don't have to follow it. But if you do things work better. Jack says it's fire insurance for the soul. But you better make up your mind before you call Cody. He will probably ask you if you are a Christian before he asks you to marry him."

She went home. On the way she thought about what Susan had said. It made her mad. To think that she had to buckle under to what Jack said or else. Then she thought about the rest and decided to talk to Jack again and went to his house with the idea of arguing about it. He could see right off what her plan was, he told her to sit down and shut up and told her it was a simple thing. All you have to do is believe that Jesus is God and say that you know you are a sinner and believe that he died for your sins and that makes you a Christian. Then ask him to forgive you for your sins. It doesn't cost you anything and it keeps you out of hell. I know that I'm not very good at telling people these things, but if you will pray a little prayer like me, it will be a sure thing. They prayed. Afterward she was over being mad at Jack. He gave her a Bible and asked her to go to church with him and Terry.

She did. After church she waited until everyone was gone and talked to Rev. Bob. She told him what had happened and asked if it was good. He said yes.

When she got through to Cody, she told him all about it. He said, "I'm glad, He's right you know we wouldn't have been able to be married without it. I'm sorry that he was so blunt about it though. He's not known for his diplomacy. I hope that he hasn't made you change your mind about marrying me."

"No, I love you, but he did make me mad. I was ready to fight. Then I talked to Susan, she said she had to be a Christian to marry her husband too. That made me calm down. But I'll admit that I was on the verge of total rebellion. So when will it happen?"

"I have four days off in three weeks. So, it needs to be then. Grandpa has the dates. Terry said she would have everything ready. All you have to do is show up. I rented a great little apartment, but if you don't like it, we can move when the lease is up."

"I'm sure it will be fine. Is Eric and Minnow coming up for the wedding?"

"Eric can't, but I think Minnow is. Call her and ask her.

Jack took Mickey to the dress shop to try on white dresses. Like Minnow she wanted one that she could wear later. The one Jack liked best, Mickey said, "too many boobs showing. I'm not Minnow you know."

Jack said, "Yea, I know, she did like to show them off. But yours are just as nice and it is your wedding. Everyone kind of expects to see them."

She picked out one a little less revealing but still very pretty.

Jack asked about Bride's maid dresses.

She said, "We can use the ones from Minnow's wedding. Minnow can fit into mine. Though it will not show enough boob to suit her."

Terry disagreed, she took Mickey and made her pick out some new Bridesmaid dresses. The shop had the right sizes. Besides Jack was paying for them they should take advantage of it.

The day came. Cody and Minnow came in on the same plane the day before. Susan's husband Don and Jack acted as grooms and Minnow and Sue as Bridesmaids. Mickey looked very beautiful and very happy too. I think Cody was in a state of shock.

At the reception, Cody thanked Jack for everything and said to send him a bill. So that he could get around to paying it someday.

The Happy couple spent the night at the Hotel. They left the next morning on the float plane for Juneau and their flight home. Minnow decided to stay a few days to visit with her family. She stopped by Jack's office. She said, "do you know what happens when a healthy young woman has sex with a healthy big man?"

"She gets pregnant?"

"That's what they say, the Doctor thinks it might be twins."

"How is Eric taking it?"

"I may have to come live with you until they are old enough to go fishing with him. No, He's OK with it. I told him that's what happens if you want sex five times a day. He said he would get fixed. Said he couldn't afford to support a whole Indian tribe."

"Well, now Cody and Mickey will probably start having Great Grandkids. There is birth control you know."

"What, you don't want Grandkids?"

"This will make sixteen if its twins. Do you know how much that costs at Christmas time?"

"You can afford it.

"My wife shops all year long to get just the right present for them all. It's going to bankrupt me."

"Quit whining, I need to borrow the Minny for today to go see my folks, OK?"

"Ask your dad if he is going to help pay for twin grandkids?"

"Good luck. You know better than that. He doesn't even want to pay for his kids."

CHAPTER 11

By the end of January there was enough snow on the ground to make anyone who liked a white Christmas happy. The snow had even piled up on the tarp on the boat. Jack climbed inside and fired up the heater and started pushing it up off the outside. They had a call from Ketchikan with a load for Juneau. But with all that snow on the tarp and Mickey gone it would be hard for Sue and him to handle the tarp. With the help of the heater, he got the snow off and they headed for Ketchikan. With the help of a dock hand, they got the tarp rolled up and tied to the boom. As soon as they were loaded, they headed NW for Juneau. With just the two of them it was the old four on and four off watches at the wheel. Jack asked Sue if she had another sister. She said yes. But she was only fifteen.

"Do you think she would like a job?"

"She would love one, but you can't work on a boat until you are sixteen. It's the law."

Jack asked, "when does she turn sixteen?"

"In March. She finished high school at Christmas. The Indian school makes sure you are done by the time you're sixteen, because everyone wants to work on the boats. And if they weren't done with school they would quit anyway."

"Is she as pretty as you?"

"Yes, we all look alike. We are sisters you know. Why aren't you out of Grandsons?"

"No, we have four more."

"Well, I have only three more sisters."

At Juneau they picked up a pallet of booze for Skagway again. They spent the night tied to the dock up there. No cruise ships that time of year.

Back at Juneau they had a load waiting for them to go to Angoon.

No load there. Jack got a call from Dave in Sitka. He said there was a small load going to Ketchikan, if they wanted it. It would just make enough to pay expenses. But they took it. From Ketchikan to Klawock and Craig. Then home for a few days. Sue took the Minny and brought back her sister whose name was Janice instead of some unpronounceable Indian name.

Sue took her to meet Jack. Jack said, "I hope you last longer than your sisters. The best plan is to not fall in love with any of my Grandsons. If you do tell them that you can't marry them until you're eighteen. Will you have another sister old enough to work by then?"

Jan laughed and said, "yes, but she wants to be a nurse."

Jack just shook his head and said, "Take her out to the boat and show her around. We head out tomorrow."

The girls were there early the next morning. Sue rowed them out to the Terry Beth and then unhooked it from the buoy and left the skiff tied there.

Jan was excited about the trip and had a lot of questions. Why on such a big boat was it powered by just one outboard. Sue answered, "The original motor was only eighty horsepower. This outboard is one hundred and fifty horsepower. We can't even run it all out if we're empty, it's too much for the hull speed." Girls growing up around boats know about hull speed.

She said, "What is the hull speed?"

"About fifteen knots."

Sue said, "here take the wheel, you might as well learn your job."

Jan was so excited that she giggled. Jack thought she was even cuter than her sisters.

They arrived at the dock at one in the afternoon and were loaded by one thirty. It was another medical load for Sitka. With Jan at the wheel and Sue making dinner, Jack was out fussing around the load making sure that all was secure, in case he decided to go out around the Islands instead of the inside passage. When he came into the cabin, Sue asked. "What was Mickey so mad about before she left? By the time I got there it was all over. I missed all the fun."

Jack said, "I told her she couldn't marry Cody unless she became a Christian. She didn't like it."

Sue said, "who said she couldn't marry Cody?"

"Me. I'm the head of my family and I don't think Cody would go against what I said anyway. Besides I paid for the wedding. Without my money there wouldn't have been a wedding."

Jan said, "what do you mean that you have to be a Christian to marry someone from your family?"

"The Bible says that you should not marry someone who is not a Christian. So, in my family it's a rule."

Jan said, "So, how do you become a Christian? You know just in case I want to marry one of your Grandsons."

Jack said, "It's not hard. You just have to believe that Jesus is God and that he died for your sins. Then ask him to forgive you of your sins and you're a Christian. You might pray a little prayer like this, dear Jesus thank you for dying for my sins. Please forgive my sins and when I die, I want to live with you, amen. That would do it. It will keep you out of Hell's fire. So, it's fire insurance for the soul. It's a personal thing between you and god."

Sue said, "If I say that prayer then I'm a Christian?"

"Yea, then you can marry one of my Grandsons."

Jan asked, "how many more do you have?"

"Five, don't worry I'll save one for you."

Sue said, "are they all as handsome as Cody?"

"They are all cousins or brothers, so, yes."

They reached home at eight and spent the night, or most of it they left at three in the morning. That got them into Sitka at nine thirty in the morning.

Jack called Dave and he came to see them at the dock. He was a little surprised to see another pretty deck hand on board.

He said, "how many good-looking girls are there in your family?"

Jan said, "there are five of us left that aren't married yet. Are you looking for a wife?"

"Well, I was going to ask Mickey to marry me, but Cody beat me to it. Who's next?"

Jack said, "If you move fast, you might get Sue here. But I have another Grandson headed this way so you better hurry."

Dave drops down on his knees and raises his hands to Sue and says, "Sue marry me. Before another Grandson shows up."

She said, "if I thought you were serious, I might say yes. But you aren't as pretty as Cody, so I think I'll wait to see what the next Grandson looks like."

They left Dave with a broken heart and headed for Juneau with a small load and got a large load for Yakutat. When they hit the open sea, the wind was picking up and it was getting dark. So, they pulled into the harbor at Pelican to spend the night. This time of year, the sun wasn't up very long anyway. It was cold enough that they had the propane heater going in the wheelhouse all the time.

Jan was the first one up. She went out to the toilet and came back in and said, "man it's cold out there I think that I have frost bite on my bottom."

Jack said, "let me see. I would be happy to warm it up for you."

Sue said, "maybe you could cut a hole through the wall to let some warm air out there. It would have to be near the ceiling to keep you from watching us go potty though."

Jack said, "you should be ashamed of yourself for thinking such evil thoughts. That's a good idea though. It is cold out there."

Jack called the Coast Guard to check on the wind. They said it was still blowing. So, they pulled the anchor and went and tied up at the city dock and the girls went to explore the town. They came back in a couple of hours with some food stuff that they were getting short of and told Jack that he should see this town That it was cute. While they were gone Jack had cut a hole through to the head right at the ceiling to let some warm air out there. He didn't want a frost bit butt either.

Jan said that she wanted to show Jack something in the town. They left Sue to guard the boat and climbed the ladder and went to see what Jan thought was so wonderful. It was a totem pole. It was impressive though.

Jan was such a young little cutie that Jack had a hard time not liking whatever she was excited about. Jack bought some ground beef and beens and made Chili for dinner. The girls said they liked it. At least it was a change from fish stew.

They pulled into Yakutat about the time it got light enough to see anything. The sun probably wasn't going to show today.

There wasn't a crane here, so they had to boom the pallets onto the dock. To be picked up. Jack trned down a load to Anchorage, It was too far in open sea. He took a small load to Juneau. It was nighttime when they reached Pelican, so they stopped for the night again. Though it was hard to tell by the daylight, since the sun didn't make it over the horizon just some daylight for a few hours around noon. Jack got a phone call from his wife about eight that night. She said, "Ryan is flying into Juneau tomorrow.

He would like to ride down with you. I told him that it sometimes took a few days and many stops. But he said that it would be fun traveling with you. He said his dad rode up from Seattle and that it was the best part of his stay. He probably told him that when Minnow wasn't around."

"What did you tell him about where to meet us?"

"I told him to take a cab to the dock and wait for you there. What time will you get there?"

"What time will he get there?"

"His flight will arrive at noon."

"We will pick him up at one. We have a load for there and will arrive about noon. But we don't unload where we would usually pick him up. There are no cruise ships there now. So, we can go right to the regular docks we'll be there at one." When he hung up, he told the girls the news. Sue looked kind of worried. Jack asked, "What's wrong with you?"

She said, "I don't have anything to wear but work clothes. Can we leave early so I can do some shopping before we pick him up?"

Jack and Jan both started laughing at the age old 'I don't have anything to wear.'

They pulled out at six in the morning. That would give her an hour to shop and get back to the boat on time.

At one, they pulled up to the dock where the cruise ships docked and there was Sue dressed in new clothes. A short tight jacket that with the bottom buttons buttoned made her shirt stick out more than usual. She was ignoring Ryan like she didn't know we were picking him up. He was not ignoring her, she looked too good.

As soon as Jan tied them off Jack climbed to the deck above and hugged Ryan. He pretended not to see Sue. He climbed down to the boat and told Ryan to pass down his bags. Sue yelled, "Captain Jack you mean old man, you are going to be sorry for this." With all the yelling Jan came out on deck and Sue threw her packages down to her. Poor Ryan was embarrassed. He didn't know what was going on. Sue climbed down onto the boat and picked

Up her things and stormed into the wheelhouse and slammed the door. Leaving Jack and Jan laughing and Ryan not getting it.

Jack introduced Jan to Ryan and went into the wheelhouse as Jan cast off. When they were moving Ryan asked Jan, "What was that all about?"

Jan felt sorry for him. She said, "She went and bought new clothes to impress you. Jack was pulling one of his jokes on her. It worked. She's mad. Sue and I are Mickey and Minnow's sisters."

"You sure look alike. You're all very pretty. Do you have more sisters?"

"Yes three, why how many Grandsons does Captain Jack have?"

"Four more, are all of the others as pretty as you four?"

"I think they are all prettier than me. But thank you. Let's go in, It's cold out here."

They had picked up a load for Sitka so were headed west. Jack was at the wheel. He turned it over to Jan and sat down with Ryan and a cup of coffee. He yelled down at Sue. "Hey, it's lunch time come make something and give Ryan a cup of coffee." She came up from below looking like nothing had happened and handed Ryan a cup of coffee. Jack said, "Oh yea this is Sue, She's first mate. You will never see a better looking first mate if you look for the rest of your life."

Ryan stood up and said to Sue "I'm sorry that Grandpa pulled one of his dumb jokes on you. He's known for them. Please don't be mad at me for it."

She smiled at him and said, "I will try to ignore him for the rest of this trip. And I will tell Terry about it."

Jack looked worried and said, "come on it was just a joke."

Sue said, "Please tell him that I warned him that he would be sorry."

Jan thought it was all funny. She didn't believe for a minute that Jack was worried or mad and she didn't think Ryan did either. She even though Sue was just playing along for the fun of it. This little scene went on for a while until Sue decided that it was cutting into her flirting time. They were running with the big flood light on up on the roof. It was going to be dark all the way to Sitka.

They got to Sitka at seven at night, so they dropped anchor. And ate dinner. Sue had the cooking done when they arrived. Ryan said that he wanted to see if her cooking was better than Minnow's. He decided that it was. At sea on a boat thing always tasted good. He knew what this 'fishing trip' was going to turn into. Both his dad and Cody had warned him, but he was already hooked. The bait was way more than he could resist, and he knew it.

They talked late into the night. Ryan told them about himself. That he had bought a house and had a good job. Sue asked about a car. He said, "I have a Honda and a Chevy truck. They are not new but are good vehicles. Minnow finally got her driver's license. She almost got in a fight with her instructor. Mickey is trying to get hers. Do you have yours Sue?"

Jack said, "There are no roads up here so just about no one has one in the Islands here. In Fairbanks and the rest of the state up North they have a few roads, so they have cars, and licenses."

Sue said, "I will get mine as soon as we are married if you buy me a car."

Jack jumped up and yelled, "who said anything about marriage? You guys have got to stop taking my crews away. The next sister is too young to work on a boat."

Ryan smiled and said, "It's your fault for hiring such pretty girls. Anyway, she hasn't asked me, yet I might say no."

Sue said, "will you marry me, Ryan?"

He said, "it was decided the first time I saw you. If you hadn't asked me, I would have asked you in the next day or so. How long does it take to get married here Grandpa?"

"As captain of the ship and as an elder of a church I could marry you tonight. But Terry would be mad at not being there. Her folks would not be happy either. Well, I'll call Terry and Susan. First though, did you say that little prayer the other day? It's a must."

Sue said, "yes I did. But you have lousy bed side manner Captain Jack. I'll call Susan and Terry. You would probably mess that up too."

CHAPTER 12

Sue and Ryan took the float plane to Petersburg the next day to get a dress bought and things started. Jack and Jan got a small load to the nurse at the Indian village. They went down the outside of the Islands to save time and arrived at the village about noon. They boomed the load onto the dock then Jan ran up to her folk's house to tell her family the news. Her dad came down to the boat. He said, "how many more Grandsons do you have?"

Jack said, "four, but your daughters are too young for them. The rest live in Idaho and all, but one is too young too. I hope I can keep Jan for a while. She is a good worker, and I can't run this boat alone."

"So, when is the wedding?"

"I don't know, I'll send you a message as soon as I hear anything."

Terry set the wedding up for Saturday night so that Eric and Minnow and Cody and Mickey could all be there. Minnow was getting big with her twins. Mickey said that she was pregnant too. Jack was happy but Terry said she was not ready to be a Great

Grandmother yet.

Rev. Bob Witcombe did a fine job marrying them. Sue had Mickey and Jan as her Bridesmaids. Eric and Cody stood up with Ryan. Jack and Terry were very proud of the whole family.

At the reception Jack danced with all four girls and his wife. She even paid for some of it. She didn't make Jack pay for all of it this time. It was Beautiful and so were the girls. Dan and Carol came too. He was doing good on his peg. He even danced with Minnow and Mickey and Terry and Carol too. Sunday morning Mickey took Eric and Cody fishing. Ryan said he was too busy. It was cold out and they decided to only get one fish each. Besides they had to get the float plane out that morning and would leave the smoking and shipping to Jack and Jan.

Ryan said, "I might go fishing later. Right now, I'm too busy, and besides it's cold outside and the sun never comes up. Him and Sue did make it out to eat a few times. They seemed to really like the inside of that hotel room.

These long dark days Jack spent working on his book. Jan kept the Terry Beth tied to the dock by Jack's house and spent a lot of time aboard running the heater to keep the pipes from freezing. The day after Ryan and Sue left, they got a call from Ketchikan. Another medical load for Sitka. They had a couple of pallets for Craig too. If they wanted them. It meant a lot of open sea because if you went around to Craig, you might as well stay out there to Sitka.

It was going to be a long lumpy trip for just the two of them and her only sixteen.

They left Ketchikan at two. It was already getting dark. they reached Craig at seven. They couldn't get unloaded until morning, so they tied up to the dock and went to a little café on the pier for supper. Jack had steak and eggs. He said he was tired of fish. Jan had fish and chips. She said it was greasy. But that she grew up on fish and that until eating his chili she could not remember the last time she had beef.

When they got back to the boat the temperature outside was ten degrees. The heater in the wheelhouse felt good. Jack said, "I always sleep in my underpants, so don't look."

She said, "me too, but you can look if you want. I grew up in a one room house with ten kids I'm used to it."

Like her sisters she wore no bra. If you think Jack didn't look, Your wrong. He looked when they got up too. They ate breakfast and went out to untie the load and get ready to unload. Then went back inside to drink coffee until someone came to except the cargo.

They boomed the two pallets to the dock and as soon as the dock hand signed for them, they pulled out and headed west out to sea then northwest up the coast to Sitka. Jack didn't know if the sea was making up or going down but the waves were at least seven feet high when they rounded the Island. The trip was a little rough though. They arrived at four in the afternoon.

The wind was only about ten knots, so the sea was not too bad. After unloading they called Dave and since they had no cargo, they found a place to tie to a dock and went to dinner with Dave at a restaurant in town. Jack ordered a roast beef dinner. Dave asked, "can Jan cook as good as her sisters? She is just as pretty."

Jack said, "yes she can cook, but she is only sixteen and if you propose to her, I'll shoot you. I'm tired of you Horney guys running off with my crews."

Jan said, "It wouldn't do any good to ask my dad says we can't get married until we are eighteen. Besides you're not as good looking like his Grandsons and he has four more to choose from."

Dave said, "I can wait two years. You are just as pretty as your sisters.

If we could make some kind of agreement now for two years from now- "

Jack said, "I'm warning you"

Jan said, "he is just kidding, I think you are getting paranoid."

"You would be too, if you lost three of your crew in so short a time."

She said, "you didn't lose them. Now they are part of your family."

Jack called the hospital. They told him that there were two pallets in Juneau to be picked up if he wanted them. And another small one to the Indians again.

Dave asked, "can I ride along, I want to try Jan's

cooking?"

Jack said, "we could use another hand. But not some horn dog after my help. So shove off."

From Juneau back to Sitka then south to the village again. Then home for a few days. The darkness was hard to deal with. You couldn't see very well even with the big flood light.

Jack was glad to be home. Jan went down to the boat a lot to make sure the heater didn't run out of gas.

Terry complained about him not being home and not helping with the housework. Jack said, "why don't you hire a maid? I need to work on my book. Hire Jan, then she won't be out of work while I write."

Terry agreed. Jack called Susan's house. He knew Susan was at work, Jan answered. He said, "my wife wants someone to clean the house one day a week. She will pay you. That way you can make a little extra when the boat isn't going out. You can even stay here to save on the rent."

She said, "you just want to see me in my underpants again. Well, OK. But I'll just work for room and board. It would be better for watching the boat and using the backhoe to clear snow too."

Jack drove her to Susan's house to get her things. It wasn't much, she didn't have many clothes. After they took them into the spare bedroom. Jack said, "I need you to come to the store with me to help pick out some things.

When they were in the store Jack told the girl clerk to get her some insulated jeans and snow boots and a couple of heavy shirts and a warm coat with a hood. Don't take no for an answer. When it was all bagged up Jan came to him and said, "this is too much Jack, people are going to think something funny is going on."

Jack said, "I better not here about it. You work for me you need warm clothes for that."

When they got home Jack helped her carry in her packages and went to his office to work on his book. Jan started putting things away. She went to his office to ask for more hangers. He said there are extra hangers in the laundry room.

Soon she was back, "where is the cleaning stuff kept at?"

He said, "ask Terry when she gets home. I'm busy."

"Can I start some dinner then?"

"Sure, but you are on your own I don't know a thing." He kept typing.

She went exploring around the kitchen until she located everything that she needed and started cooking. She baked some sour dough bread and made smoked fish stew. When Terry came home, she walked into the kitchen and said, "Jan, it smells so good that I thought Minnow was back. Did Jack tell you to make dinner? He likes that fish stew."

Jan said, "he moved me in here, and I needed

something to do so I cooked. I hope it's all right."

"Well, I hate to cook. So, if you are going to live here and like to cook, I would really like it. Is the room, OK?"

"We grew up in a one room house with ten kids. To have a room of my own is wonderful. I hope that it's OK for you."

"If you are going to clean house and cook too. I will be glad to pay you to live here."

It was snowing when Jan went to the boat in the morning. The heater was out of propane. So, she changed tanks and then Jack showed up and it took them more than an hour to get the tarp off the boom and hooked onto the hooks. By then they were both cold and ready for some coffee. They went to the house. Jack had put the coffee on before he left. It and they were ready. Jack said, "The money you make plowing snow is all for you. Just keep the gas tank full. Dress warm, there is no heater on the tractor.

CHAPTER 13

Jan kept busy plowing snow and cooking and cleaning. She came to Jack's office with two cups of coffee and sat and watched him work. After a while he said, "did you want something, or are you just visiting?"

"Just visiting, I was getting lonely. You weren't around telling stories. Do you have some books that you wrote, I would like to just sit here and read I don't like to be alone?"

"Yea, on the shelf behind you. You might like the ghost story. It's the one with the three musketeers on the front. It's a book of short stories. You will like it."

He wrote and she read. When it was time, she went to the kitchen and started cooking dinner. She only knew how to fix fish. That is all they had at her home.

Jack said, "look, you are a good cook, but I want some beef now and then. Let's go to the store. I will show you what to buy and teach you how to cook it."

He showed her how to pick out a good roast and some steaks and some ground beef. He told her what to buy for trimmings and what spices to use.

He wrote down the recipe for his favorite chili. It's a good thing they took the truck, they needed it.

It snowed for three days. Almost three feet. Which brought the level up to almost five feet? Jack and Jan went down every day to push the snow off the tarp. You got under the tarp and pushed up and the snow would slide off right there, so you kept moving.

Jan plowed snow and Jack wrote. When Jan wasn't busy, she sat in Jack's study reading and keeping their coffee cups full. The quiet wasn't going to last though. Two days after the snow quit, Ketchikan called. The dock foreman said, "you guys have been laying around long enough. I have a full load for you. Be here in the morning. I have cargo for Craig, Klawock, Wrangell and Juneau. A full load." So, they loaded supplies and left. It would be a few days trip. Jack felt that his butt had grown into his office chair anyway. It was time for some action.

When the first guy arrived at the dock in Ketchikan, Jan smiled really nice and asked, "would you help us a minute." He wanted to sign on for life but when the tarp was secured his boss yelled for him to get to work and he left. The crane lowered the pallets onto the boat, all they had to do was tie them down and cover them. It was cold out and it felt good to get underway, so they could be in the warm wheelhouse. It was a six-hour trip to Craig. With Jack at the wheel Jan was reading one of Jack's books. She stopped reading and was sitting thinking, she asked, "in your spy story, you have a Moslem girl become a

Christian. Do people really change religion so easily?"

"If someone kills your father because of some small religious difference, I think you would want to change. The big thing there was that she was marrying a Jew. Her being a Moslem Made the two people's enemies. They could never go back to Israel. They would be hated by their own families."

"I guess I need to know more about being a Christian."

"There is a bible on the shelf over there. Read the first twenty verses of the book of John."

She got the Bible and he told her how to find John. She sat down and read. She read the whole book. Stopping now and then to ask a question, like, "this says that Jesus created everything. Do you believe that?"

"Whatever it says I believe."

They made it to Craig by one thirty and unloaded one pallet there and moved across to Klawock and unloaded two pallets there. Then left for Wrangell. Jack called Dan and told him that they would be there by eight. If he and Carol wanted to eat dinner that late, he would buy. Dan agreed and said that they would meet them at the café.

They tied up at the city dock just before eight and made it to the café right at eight. Dan was excited about getting a job at the Hardware store. He said, "now when her time gets close Carol can quit to take care of the baby. I don't make a lot of money, but we'll make it."

Carol said, "I can work part time in the afternoon shift if I have to. I would rather do that than be broke all the time."

Jack said, "I think I can come up with some baby furniture. It was for me so it's kind of old, but it is still in good shape." They knew it would be new stuff and laughed at him. Dan asked how everybody was doing. Jan said, "Jack made all of us become Christians."

Dan said, "he can't make you do it."

She said, "he wouldn't pay for their weddings if they didn't."

Carol said, "I guess he can make you. He is a bit sneaky."

"I didn't say I wouldn't pay for their weddings. She is making that up."

"He didn't have to say it. We got the message."

Carol said, "You too Jan? You're not getting married too, are you?"

"I was there when Sue did it, so I did too. No, I'm not getting married, but I have been asked."

Jack said, "You remember Dave, He missed out with Mickey and Sue, so he is trying with Jan. If he wasn't so ugly, he may have beat out the grandsons, but that's life."

Carol said, "he isn't ugly. But he is unemployed, and women want security. The grandsons have jobs."

Dan said, "I have a job now and with my disability we can have a little security. And even eat regular without Carol bringing home scraps from the restaurant."

Carol said, "I think all men are liars. Or maybe it's just ex-service men."

Jack said, "I think women expect us to lie. They ask for it with questions like, does this dress make me look fat? Or how do you like my new hairdo? Or do you think she is prettier than me?" Everybody laughed.

Carol looked at Dan and said, "Jack's wife is not here so he's safe. But your wife is here so you better keep your mouth shut." More laughter.

Jan said, "If this kind of stuff goes on all the time when you're married, maybe I'll hold off until I become a better fighter."

Dan said, "Do you have something for the Hardware store?"

"Yea, and the tide will be high in the morning so we will boom it to the dock early. You can pick it up there by six. We have a load for Juneau and want to get an early start. It takes all day to get there."

"OK, I'll be at the dock at six. How do you like working on the boat Jan?"

"I love it. I will miss it when I get married."

Jack growled and said, "When she quits, I'm going to sell the boat and just write."

Dan said, "Do you do pretty good? I would like

to do something like that if it pays enough to support a family."

"We charge less than the steam ships. So, we get all the work we want. We do pretty well. If you're serious start saving your money. She will leave me in two years."

"How much do you want for her?"

"I have about six thousand in it. It would be nice to get that back."

"Do you think your wife could come up with a loan?"

"Just save your money. However, much you save will be the down payment. I'll carry the rest."

So, the future of the boat was settled. But not yet.

In the morning, Dan was early, and they got unloaded and were gone before six. They stopped at Petersburg for fuel and kept going. They reached Juneau at three and they had a load for Yakutat, so when they were loaded, they headed for Pelican to spend the night. Jack pulled up to the dock and Jan got out to borrow a skiff. She tied it on and climbed back aboard. They anchored out and rowed ashore and went up to the restaurant for dinner. At dinner Jan said, "Today is my birthday, I'm seventeen and Next week my sister Karen will be sixteen. When we get near home again, we could pick her up. Then there would be two pretty girls that you could see in their underpants. Besides this four on and four off is getting old."

"Birthday huh, I see the store next door is still open. After we eat, we'll go there and buy you a present."

"We need a few things too. You know, I have always wanted a watch. Maybe we can find one cheap enough so I could have one for a present."

It was a general store, and they had some watches, none were very expensive. So, Jack told her to pick out the one she wanted. They got the other things they needed and went back to the skiff. They piled in and rowed out to the Terry Beth and got ready for bed. Before she took her clothes off, she gave Jack a big hug and said, "Thank you Jack, this is not only my first watch, but also the first birthday present that I ever got."

"If Karen's birthday is next week, we should buy her a present too. What do you think she would like? She will need clothes too."

"We can take her to the store in Petersburg, there are some things she always wanted there. She can try on her clothes there too. It will be fun. We are so poor that all we had to wear was hand me downs. All of us girls love you for being so generous. Will it be OK if Karen stays with us at your house too?"

"Sure, we can get two single beds and get her a dresser too."

"We slept in one bed at home. All of us girls together. The bed is fine."

She took a little longer getting into bed than normal.

Jack woke up to the smell of coffee and pancakes cooking. It was early but they needed to get an early start.

The sea outside was pretty flat and they made Yakutat by two. For the first time there was a pallet for Juneau. They arrived there at three in the morning and anchored out to wait for the dock workers to arrive. Jan was already asleep. But Jack got her up to take the wheel while he went out and dropped the hook. She at least put on a shirt then went back to bed. Jack set the alarm and went to bed too.

When they unloaded, they picked up a load of medical supplies for Sitka.

The hospital had a small pallet for the Indians. Jack called Dave and asked if he wanted to have dinner with them? They met him at the restaurant. Jack told Dave that it was Jan's birthday. He said, "Happy birthday, this means I have only one more year to wait. Right?"

Jan said, "you haven't seen Karen yet, she is coming to work for us as soon as we get back. She is even prettier than me."

"How old is she?"

"Well, you will have to wait for two years for her. But she's the prettiest of us all."

Dave groaned and Jack chuckled, and Jan kept telling him what a nice figure she had and what a great personality too. Poor Dave was in pain.

They pulled out early and went out to see. The

wind was up a little and the swells were about six feet but they were going with them, so they just surfed along and made the village by noon. When the medical supplies were unloaded on the dock. Jan went up to her father's house to get her sister. Her dad came down to the boat to talk to Jack. He said, "Karen won't be sixteen for two days. So, she can't work on the boat until then."

Jack said, "we don't have any work for a few days. We plan to just rest up a few days. Maybe go fishing." He just nodded his head and walked back up the hill. In a little while Jan came down to the boat with Karen in tow. Karen didn't have anything with her when she climbed aboard.

Jack said, "what no clothes."

Karen looked ashamed. Jan said, "she didn't have much, I told her to give the stuff to our sisters. That we would buy her some new stuff when we got to town."

Jack said, "Yea you have to have some warm clothes for working on the boat. It gets cold at sea especially at this time of year. Cast off Jan and show Karen around. We will make port before the store closes. We can get Karen some Duds tonight."

On the way home it started to snow. As soon as they tied to Jack's dock, Karen helped Jan and him to get the tarp spread and tied down.

They walked to the house and Jack unlocked the door. Terry wasn't home yet. They went out to his truck and drove to the store.

CHAPTER 14

While Jan helped Karen pick out clothes, Jack looked at guns in the sporting goods department. He told the man there that he wanted a 357 that would hold up on the boat. The salt air makes everything rust. He sold him a chrome plated one with a shoulder holster. Jack called Terry and said they were home and would she like to meet them at the restaurant for dinner. She said she was glad to. She was getting tired of her own cooking. Jack told Karen to put on some new clothes, they were going out to dinner. Jack bought her a suitcase for all the clothes to go home in. He went to the furniture store next door and bought her a dresser too. He took a tarp from under the back seat and covered the dresser in the back of the truck. And they went to dinner. Terry came in right after them and Jan introduced her to Karen to her. Terry said, "wow, another pretty sister, this makes five. How many more are there?"

Jan said, "just one more. Thank you for saying we are pretty."

"I have never seen five sisters before where all of them are pretty.

Jan said, "Karen is the quiet one. The rest of us are loud mouths. But you won't even know she's around. Saying that, Is it OK if she moves in with us?"

"I'm sure Jack has said it was all right. You don't need my permission. We let him think he's the boss." After dinner they went home and moved Karen in with Jan, dresser, clothes and all. Jack went to his office to work on his books and his book.

In the morning the snow was a foot deep. Jan went out early with Karen to show her how to run the backhoe to clear snow for people. It snowed all day, so they went to the boat and cleaned the snow off the tarp twice during the day. It snowed all night and the next day too. Karen had never driven anything before, so it took her a while to get the hang of driving the tractor with the clutch and all the levers. But Jan was surprised how fast that she caught on.

She told Jack, "Karen did good on the tractor. She only hit two cars all day."

"I didn't hit anything. It is fun to drive. Would you teach me to drive the truck?"

"Me too please." Said Jan

Jack said, "Yea, when we get time. The truck is easier than the tractor. No clutch to deal with." It quit snowing that afternoon and the girls finished clearing driveways before dinner time.

When Karen's birthday came along, they had a party. It was the first party she had ever had. After dinner when Jan brought out the cake and presents

Karen cried. Jan told Jack and Terry, "this is the first birthday party she has ever had. I know that's kind of sad, but we were very poor and there are too many kids. It was my first party last week. Jack bought me a watch and took me out to dinner. It was my first watch too."

Terry said, "you girls don't usually stay with us long enough to have two birthday parties."

Jan said, "That is your fault for having so many handsome sons and

Grandsons. We can't help ourselves."

Two days later jack got a call from Ketchikan. They had freight for Sitka, and Juneau. The snow had stopped. They rolled up the tarp and lashed it to the boom. Gassed up and left at ten o'clock so they could be at the dock in Ketchikan when they opened for business. The girls slept all the way.

The sun was up longer now so you could see better during the day.

Jack had them load the Sitka pallets first because he thought he would go to Juneau first. They might have something for Sitka too.

Jan took the wheel when they left. She let Karen take over when it got lighter. Jack slept since he had the wheel all night. He told Jan to stop in Kake when they got there, they would spend the night.

Jan didn't wake him up until her and Karen had tied to the dock at Kake.

Jack combed his hair and put on his Captain hat, and they went up to the café for dinner. At dinner Karen said, "I could get used to this eating out all the time. It's hard to remember eating anything that we didn't have to cook first."

Jack said, "well since you like it so much, you pay the bill."

"I don't have any money, and if you take all of those clothes that you bought me out of my pay, I won't have any for about a year."

"Those are free, we can't have you running around naked this time of year." When Jack paid for dinner, he did it with a fifty-dollar bill. A man standing nearby saw that he had more and when they left and headed for the boat they were followed. Once they were aboard Jack and Jan went into the wheelhouse. Karen started to cast off the lines. A man jumped into the boat and grabbed Karen and put a gun to her head and told her to yell. She did. Jack came out of the wheelhouse with a 357 and shot the man holding Karen. The other two men on the dock shot at him. Hitting him in the left arm and shoulder. He went down but returned their fire. All the shooting brought some people including the local cop. He asked what happened. Karen in a shaky voice told him. Jan was busy patching Jack up. Trying to stop the bleeding. The cop said, "three dead men with three shots while he's under fire, that's some shooting."

Jan looked up from working on Jack and said, "he was a marine and an expert shot. You don't mess with

Captain Jack."

The cop said, "the closest hospital is at Sitka. You better take him there. A couple of you guys drag the dead guy off the boat so they can get going. When you're in the area again stop by and fill out a report. This is the first shooting we've had in a while we're going to need the details."

Jack was awake but they had to help him into the wheelhouse. He told them to set up a cot in there for him and put a tarp over it so he wouldn't bleed on the bedding down below. They took off for Sitka. Jan was at the wheel. Karen took off her bloody shirt and had to wash her hair in the sink. Jack's bullet had splattered her pretty good with the robber's blood. She was drying her hair with a towel when she saw that Jack was watching her, she didn't have anything on above the belt. She said, "I thought you were out you dirty old man."

"I'm the Captain, I have to keep an eye on what goes on with this boat."

Jan said, "he is a man, even if he's old you can't expect him to be any different than the rest." Karen went down and put on a clean shirt and came up and made coffee. It was a six-hour ride to Sitka.

Jack was starting to doze off when Karen brought some blankets and a pillow and covered him up. She lifted his head and put the pillow under it.

Jan said, "I hope you don't think you will get this kind treatment all the time."

Jack wasn't feeling too good, but he grinned and said, "you mean I won't see Karen with her shirt off all the time?"

"I guess that's up to Karen, but I wouldn't count on it." Jan said.

"You might want to turn on the flood light, so you don't run into someone."

"I can run the boat. You go to sleep. Besides there's a full moon." But she turned on the light.

Jan let Karen take the wheel for a while. She needed to learn to handle the boat at night. Growing up around boats, she knew about buoys. Jan was worried about Jack. With his two bullet holes and the loss of blood. The dirty old man even wounded he makes jokes about seeing Karen with her shirt off.

As they neared Sitka, Jan called the Hospital and asked them to have an ambulance on the dock waiting when they arrived. She told them that Captain Jack had been shot by bandits. They asked what his blood type was was. She woke Jack up and asked him. It was A. While Karen tied up to the dock, two guys with a stretcher came aboard and lifted Jack onto it. He was too weak to walk. The girls helped lift him onto the dock. When the ambulance left Jan grabbed a skiff and tied it on and they moved the Terry Beth out and anchored it in the bay. They rowed back and walked to the hospital. When they asked at the desk about Jack the nurse said that they needed to fill out some paperwork. It asked about insurance. Jan told the nurse that the cards were in his wallet, if she would bring his wallet, she would get them for her. The nurse started to argue but just then a doctor came in. He said, "don't worry about the paperwork right now we know these people they haul our medical supplies for us. We'll do the paperwork later."

Jan asked, "how is he?"

"He's in surgery, but he will make it. He's too tough to die. You can see him in about an hour. Get some sleep."

A reporter for the local paper showed up and asked for an interview. Jan said, "sure, get out your little tape recorder and get ready for a real story of heroism." Karen sat and listened. She was amazed. She didn't know that Jan was such a storyteller. She couldn't wait to tell Jack what a hero he was.

When they got into see Jack, he told them to go back to the boat and when the dock opened to unload the cargo for here. That he would call his wife and tell her what happened. Karen said, "tell her not to believe the story in the paper. That's Jan's version and it isn't very close to the truth. For instance, were you a Marine sniper?"

Jack said, "I was a radio operator."

Jan said, "it's my story and I'm sticking to it."

Jack said, "here is some money the doctor got it out of my pants. I think he took a couple of hundred out of it but that should get you by. When you get unloaded here go to Juneau and unload the rest there.

If you don't think you can handle it by yourselves don't take any more cargo. Just come back here. I should be ready to go in a couple of days."

The doctor said, "It may be a bit longer than that and I only took a hundred."

Jack waited until morning to call his wife. She was not going to like the idea that he killed those guys, or that he got shot. Mostly that he was in a gun battle on the dock with the whole town knowing about it. What will people say. She always got up at six, so he waited until six thirty. When she answered he said, "hi honey, there has been a little thing that happened to me. I'm in the hospital in Sitka. I will be here a few days so if you wanted to come sees me you could take some money out of my account and fly up on the float plane. Oh, don't believe the story in the paper. It's just Jan's imagination. Here is the doctor he'll tell his side of it." The doctor tells her that jack was shot and that they had to give him some blood but that he would be OK in a week or so. No, the girls weren't hurt although Jan should feel guilty about the story, she told the paper. Jack says some of it is true but not much. He hands the phone back to Jack. She said, "I'm coming up there. Maybe I can get the truth out of Karen." She hung up.

Jack went to sleep. When he woke up Terry was sitting there reading the paper. She looked up from the paper and when she saw that he was awake, she said, "you killed three men?"

"Seemed like the right thing to do at the time.

They were shooting at me, and one had a gun to Karen's head."

"What were they after?"

"We didn't have any long conversations. Maybe rape, maybe murder, robbery, I don't know. When the shooting was over no one was left alive to ask. I was laying on the deck bleeding to death and didn't care much what their reason was."

"The doctor said that Jan got you patched up enough to get you here alive. How long did it take to get here from where it happened?"

"Six hours. I don't think I could have got here any faster. There was no plane available."

"Are you worried about friends or families coming after you?"

"No, the cop came here to get a report. He said that no one seemed to know any of them. I am worried about the girls out there on the boat alone though."

"Jan has your shoulder holster with the new 357 and Karen has your 38. I think they are hoping for some trouble."

"Wild Indians. Are they running cargo?"

"No, but they did unload the stuff at Juneau and came back. They are waiting to see you."

Terry went out and brought them in. Jan was all excited. She said,

"We are famous now. All the sudden everybody has

cargo for us. When are you getting out of here?"

"The doctor says about a week, I do need some rest, so it will be a few days."

The doctor came in then and said, "the nurse said she thinks you two are packing guns. You're not supposed to carry guns in a hospital."

Jan said, "We don't have a good place to leave them."

"You can leave them in my office until you're ready to leave."

"We'll leave now. We need Jack. Can't he just ride along. We'll take good care of him. He just will rest, I promise."

"No, he needs us for a while. Come ask in a week."

"Jack told us not to worry about hauling cargo, but there is a lot of it, so I think we'll go do some work."

They picked up a load in Juneau for Sitka and a pallet for Yakutat. Then back to Juneau. From there to Angoon. After unloading in Angoon, they returned to Sitka.

They went to the hospital to see Jack and run into the Doctor.

Jan held out her coat and said, "See no guns. We came to see Jack and take him with us."

"Let's go see Jack. He is getting restless." They went to Jack's room. When they walked in, he said, "it's about time you showed up. I was getting worried that you might have sold my boat and went to Hawaii."

Jan said, "that old scow wouldn't bring enough to pay for the airfare. Are you ready to go yet?"

"I been ready since I ate my first meal here. Man, I miss your cooking."

The Doctor asked, "are they good cooks?"

"Let me out of here and you can come out to the boat for dinner tonight."

"I can't get off. But you could bring me some."

The girls went ahead and rowed out and brought the boat to the dock. The ambulance brought Jack to the dock, and he climbed aboard without help. One of the girls heated up a dish of smoked fish stew and sent to the Doctor.

The hospital had a pallet of supplies for the Indians, so they headed for home. The sea wasn't running too high, and they were going with the waves, so it was a pleasant trip to the Indian village. While they were unloading the girl's dad came down to the boat. He said, "I read in the paper that you had some trouble last week. Are my girls safe?"

"Yea, nobody was shooting at them. Jan was the one who talked to the reporter, so you can understand how much of the story in the paper is true."

"It said that you were in a gun battle with three gunmen, is that part true?"

"Yea, but I lived through it. They didn't though."

"What were they after?"

"There wasn't any conversation before the shooting started. And no one was left alive to ask afterwards. So, I don't know." He just walked away.

It was good to be home once the Terry Beth was tied up, they walked up to the house. Jack thought it seemed longer than usual. Terry met them at the door. She said, "I'm glad you came home. I have been getting a lot of phone calls about you are shooting up Kake. Some western magazine wants to interview you. You know the John Wayne of the north stuff."

"Tell them to talk to Jan she's a much better storyteller than me."

Jack got a call from Ketchikan he got orders to be there in the morning.

At dinner that night, Jack said, "We have to leave by eleven tonight. Since I'm not doing too good, you girls are going to have to do most of the driving."

Jan said, "It's all right, we are just glad to have you with us. So, you can buy us dinner and gas for the boat and give us protection from the bad men."

Karen said, "It is nice to have a Marine sniper along in case of trouble."

The girls took turns at the wheel and Jack slept. When they tied up at the dock the foreman came down and said, "Boy you guys are famous all over the Islands. Everybody wants to ship with you just so they can say they did. You have two pallets of medical stuff for Sitka. A pallet for Wrangell, two for Juneau and one for Hoogah. How are you feeling Jack?"

Jack said, "I feel good enough to chase these two girls all over the boat on the way north."

Jan said, "don't listen to this old wind bag. He slept all the way here and I was at the wheel with my shirt off."

Jack called Dan before they left Ketchikan and told him they had some stuff for him and would be there at one. How about lunch? So, Karen took the wheel. It was staying light longer, and Jan had stayed at the wheel all night. She was sleeping. Karen hadn't got a lot of sleep, but it was at least light enough. After a few hours when Jack got up to go to the head, she asked if he would stay awake and talk to her to keep her awake. He said, "I'll tell you a story, When Eric was three, He and I were in a drug store doing some shopping. He was looking at some toys on one side of a counter and I felt the need to pas' gas, so I walked around the other side of the counter not knowing that he had followed me. I looked around to make sure no one was close enough to here and let her rip. Eric slugged me in the bus and said loud enough for everyone in the store to here, 'Papa you bad boy you poo-pooed in your pants.' I looked around and everyone was grinning at me. I grabbed his hand and ran." When Karen got through laughing, she said, "you are a good storyteller. It's no wonder you write books. Is that a true story?"

"Yes, it was the most embarrassing moment of my life. Well one day at church I was having some gas trouble and after church an old lady asked my wife, 'does your husband suffer from a gas problem?' my wife said, 'no he enjoys it. That was embarrassing too."

Karen said, "you do fart more than anyone I ever knew. But I agree with your wife I think you enjoy it."

Jan came up from below saying, "what's all the laughing about?"

"Jack's farts." Karen said.

Jan said, looking at her watch, "You can get some sleep. It will be about two hours before we get to Wrangell. Now tell me your story so I can laugh."

Jack took the wheel when they arrived at Wrangell. Jan got Karen out to help unload the hardware onto the dock. Dan was there with a truck. They boomed the pallet onto the truck and went to lunch. Carol was working but took time to sit and talk after she took their order. She said, "I hear that the girls have moved in with you. Is that OK with Terry, having two pretty girls living there?"

"She loves it they do all the cooking and most of the cleaning. She complains when they are not there."

"Did Dan tell you, we're pregnant."

Dan said "I was waiting for you to tell them. I didn't want to steal your surprise."

Jack said "well congratulations, I am really happy for you. Are you going to name it Jack if it's a boy?"

Jan said, "don't do that It's sure to bring bad luck to the poor kid."

Carol said, "we are going to name him Jack. It goes good with Petrovitch. And we owe a lot to Jack, he's, our friend."

"Thank you, Carol, I consider you two my first friends in Alaska. And I love you both."

Jan said, "now isn't that sweet. You're done eating, pay the bill and let's shove off we have a long night ahead of us." Jack stands up, shakes Dan's hand, and hugs Carol, pays the bill, says goodbye and they leave.

Jack stands the first watch at the wheel. Even though he is still weak. He lets the girl's sleep. He pulled in at Petersburg and tied up to his own dock by himself and went home to sleep. He was up at six and at the dock at seven. He cast off and started the engine and was heading out when Jan came up from below. She said, "Did you go home?"

"Yes, it wouldn't do any good to arrive in Juneau at two in the morning. You can go back to sleep I'll wake you at ten. You will have eight hours sleep that way."

At ten he woke Jan and told her to wake Karen at two and him at six.

They arrived at the dock in Juneau at seven. They were unloaded right away and picked up another pallet for Sitka. They arrived in Hoogah just after nine and were on their way by ten. They got to Sitka at two in the afternoon. While the girls got unloaded, Jack went to the hospital to get checked out. The Doctor said, "well, you look pretty good for such an old man. How do you feel?"

"I'm still a little weak. I can only stand watch for four or five hours and I'm all in."

"You shouldn't be standing any watch yet. It's too soon after getting shot. That one wound was almost fatal."

"Well, if you have some supplies for the Indians we'll go home for a couple of days. My editor is complaining about me not writing enough."

They got a pallet for the Indians and left for home. With Jack not doing any watches. They tied up at Jacks dock at seven thirty and went home.

The girls cleaned house and cooked and took the speed boat to see their folks. Jack worked on his book. It didn't last long though. Only two days.

Ketchikan called. The dock foreman said, "since you guys are heroes now everybody want to ship with you. Come on down."

Karen and Jan got home in time to fix supper. While eating Jack told them, "We need to leave again tonight by midnight. We have loads for all over. Craig, klawock, Juneau and Sitka." They packed their bags and said goodbye to Terry and went aboard to get a few hours' sleep.

Jack took the first watch and woke Jan at three. Karen was up making breakfast at six. They tied up to the dock at seven They were loaded and on their way by eight. They went down around what was called Totem Island and up past Hydaburg and tied up at Craig at two. They unloaded there and were across to

Klawock by three. There was only one pallet to take off there and they headed for home. They were home by ten. They all took showers and went to bed. Jack got them up at three. He wanted to be in Juneau by noon. Jan took the first watch. Jack told her to wake him at seven. Karen got up at nine and made breakfast. She asked, "you told my sisters how to become Christians. How about me?" Jack told her to get out his Bible and told her to look up Romans. He told her the verses. Three twenty-three, then six twenty-three, five eight and nine, ten nine and ten. He said, "we are sinners, the wage of sin is death, while we were still sinners Christ died for us. If you believe that he is God and say so, then you are a Christian. Say this prayer with me. Thank you, Jesus, for dieing for my sins. Please let me come stay with you when I die." She said the prayer. She smiled and said, "Thank you Jack, I feel good. I would like to buy a Bible for myself. Are there any rules?"

"Yea, ten of them. But Jesus gave us some more. To love everyone, even your enemies. And especially your Captain."

"You didn't have to through that in, I already love you Like a father and as a friend. I'm going to start going to church when we are in port too."

They unloaded in Juneau by noon and picked up two more pallets for Sitka they borrowed a skiff and anchored out and went shopping. Jack bought both Jan and Karen Bibles and had their names printed on them. They took a cab out to Wallmart. The girls bought some clothes to go to church in. And some shoes.

They ate dinner in a nice restaurant in their new clothes. After dinner the girls changed back into work clothes, and they went back to the Terry Beth.   got there to wait for the dock to open.

They tied up to the dock at seven and while the girls got the cargo off Jack walked up to the hospital to get a checkup.

The Doctor said, "How are you doing Jack? The wound looks good. I'll take the stitches out today."

"I was feeling a little week when I was here last. But I'm fine now."

"I was worried about you when you were here last. You didn't look good. You need red meat when you have blood loss. Fish don't make it. I know those girls are good at cooking fish but buy some beef."

"I have been teaching them how to cook beef. They are quick learners.

"How are the girls working out on the boat?"

"They're doing good. When not on watch they clean it, and the food is great."

"I think I'll leave the stitches on your back until next trip. It looks good but that was a big hole, and I don't want it to break open again. Another week won't hurt you anyway."

"OK you're the doctor. I'll see you in a week or so."

The dock had two pallets for Juneau, so they left right away when Jack got back to the boat.

Juneau had two pallets for Yakutat. So, they spent the night at Pelican again. They ate dinner at the café in town that night.

When they came out of the café there were three men standing around talking by the door one of them said, "Are you the ones who shot up the dock at Kake a while ago?" Jack was going to try to lie out of it, but Jan pulled out a gun and said, "Yea, do you want see us shoot up the dock here too. The three guys who started it down there are dead you know."

The three guys just mumbled something and left in a hurry.

Jack said, "are you trying to start a fight?"

"I didn't get to shoot anybody the last time. I was ready this time."

They left Pelican at midnight so they could get into Yakutat in the morning when the dock hands arrived. There wasn't any cargo for them there, so they went back to Juneau. In the morning they got a load for Sitka and at Sitka the hospital had a pallet for the Indians and so they went home.

Being Saturday night, they decided that they would all go to church the next day. The girls with their new Bibles in their new church clothes riding in Terry's new all-wheel drive Honda.

Even Jack got dressed up in a suit. They all looked good.

Rev Bob Witcombe met them at the door and Jack told him quietly that Karen just accepted the lord. Rev. Bob told the people during the service and Karen was all smiles. After the service a lot of people stopped by to congratulate her. On the way home she asked, "is it all right for Indian girls to go to a white man's church?"

Terry said, "in God's eyes we are all the same. We are all his children. There is an old song that goes, Red and yellow, Black and white they are precious in his sight, all the little children of the world."

During lunch Jack said, "I think we should join that church. I like his preaching and we are home at least a couple of Sundays a month. Enough that we could be considered regular members. What do you think?"

Terry said, "I like that church. I would like that. The girls would have to be baptized first. You better explain that to them first."

Jack explained about baptism to them and called Rev. Bob and told him that they wanted to join the church. But the girls needed to be baptized. Would he set it up? He would be glad to. He would call him with a date.

They left Tuesday night on another run from Ketchikan to Juneau. From Juneau to Yakutat. Then to Sitka. And Jack went to see the Doctor while the girls unloaded. The Doctor said, "Well, let's take out your stitches, it looks like it's healing good. How do you feel? Is there much pain left in the wound?"

"No, Movement is a little stiff yet, but it's all right."

"That's good. Say, there is something that I have been meaning to talk to you about. I know that you are not Jan's father, but she acts like you are. Do you think it would be all right for me to ask her out?"

"How old are you doc? You know that she's only eighteen?"

"Yea, I know, but I also know that you are fifteen years older than your wife. I'm only seven years older than her."

"Are you sure you want to go out with that wild cat? She pulled a gun on a guy last week outside of a restaurant who was getting smart with us."

"That is part of her charm, and she is so pretty too. That I'd like to try."

"If you have something for the Indian village. We will lay over until morning. You can take us all to dinner tonight and see how it goes. I'll tell her to dress up, that way she won't be carrying her gun. And since we are all going, she won't refuse."

So, they made a time and place to meet, and Jack left.

When Jack got back to the boat, he told the girls not to cast off, that the hospital had a pallet of stuff for the village, and they had to wait for it.

Then he told them that the Doctor was taking them to dinner at a fancy restaurant, So they all had to dress up. They both said that they didn't bring any dress up clothes. Jack gave them some money and said go buy some, we have time if you hurry. They were back in time and went below to change. Jack thought they looked great. Except that Terry would never let Jan wear that dress to church. Too much boob showing. He left the girls on the dock, borrowed a skiff and anchored out. He rowed back in, and they left for the restaurant. The Doctor, whose name was Jim Heart, ran into them on the way. He said, "Wow, you all look good. I didn't know that a bunch of sailors could look so good."

Jan said, "Thank you, I didn't know that hauling freight for you got us invited to dinner. It hasn't happened before."

"I didn't know how good you looked all dressed up before."

Once they had ordered, Jim decided to ask her if he could ask her out.

He said, "I know this is a bit strange, but I would like to date you Jan. I know that I'm older than you, but I like you a lot, and I would like to get to know you better."

She looked at him a long time. Then said, "I like you too Doc. But you are way out of my class. You know that I'm an Indian, right? With no education to speak of. And a nature wilder than most men?"

"I know all that. But you are the most exciting woman I've ever met."

"Well, I have to ask, what are your intentions? Is this just for sex, or is this serious?"

"I'm serious."

Jack said, "why don't you take some time off and ride down with us. You can use the excuse that you need to check on the nurse at the village. You might even do a little doctoring while you're there."

"That's a good idea Jack. I've never been there. And the nurse could use my help."

"And the girls are getting baptized this Sunday. It's an occasion that you might like to see. You can take the float plane home when you want. And you can meet her folks."

Karen said, "That might dampen your enthusiasm. That old man is mean all the time. Jack is only mean sometimes."

CHAPTER 15

They picked the Doc up at the dock with his bags at six in the morning and headed out to sea. The sea was mostly calm, so they rode the lump down the coast and docked up at the village at one in the afternoon. Doctor Jim helped boom the pallet over onto the dock while Karen went up to see her folks and tell her dad to come meet the doc. It had been a while since they had seen a doctor so the whole family came down to the boat. Karen introduced everyone and waited with a big grin on her face for the doctor to speak. He said, "I am very glad to meet all of you, Is everyone in good health?"

Karen's dad said, "We're in good health. Have good nurse."

"Well, I'm glad to hear that. I have another reason for coming here. I wanted to ask if I could date your daughter."

"Karen too young for you."

Jan speaks up and said, "come on dad you know he means me."

"You are crazy if you marry her she wild Indian.

She liable to scalp you in your sleep."

You could tell that it shook the Doc up. But he said, "I'll take my chances anyway Karen said she would protect me." They all laughed.

Jack said, "the girls are getting baptized Sunday. Would you like to come?"

"They let Indians in white man church?"

"In Gods eyes we're all the same. You could even come join. Do you have a church here in the village?"

"No need one no Christians here."

Jan said, "mom is one and so are the little kids in your house and all of us girls are too. You are the only heathen."

The old man just grunted and walked home with the rest of the family going with him.

The nurse asked Doctor Jim to look at a couple of her patients before they left. But they were still home by three in the afternoon. Jack told the Doctor that he could sleep on the couch, or on the boat, or he could get a hotel room. His choice. Jan drove him down to the hotel and got him checked in and brought him back to stay with them for dinner. He wanted to stay for some their famous smoked fish stew. After dinner Terry asked them if they wanted to play some games. Jan liked Mexican train. During the game Terry asked Jim how he liked the ride down and the village. He answered, "It was exciting Jan even let me steer the boat. I would really like to take the time to make a full trip with them some time."

In the morning they met Jim at the restaurant for breakfast and then walked to church together.

The girls brought some old clothes to get baptized in. No white shirts that you can see through when they are wet.

Rev. Bob met them at the door, and after introductions, he took the girls bag of clothes and told them to come forward to the front at the invitation. As they went in Jack explained about the invitation. Karen said, "do we have to go down front?"

Jack said, "Terry and I will go with you. We have to anyway."

After the service, when Rev. Bob said for everybody to bow their heads. He asked if anyone wanted to except the lord, that they should come forward and someone would pray with them. And if anyone wanted to join the church they should come forward now to. Jack and Terry and the girls all stood up and started down the aisle. The Doctor stayed seated. When they got to the front, the rev. told them to come up on the stage and turned them around to face the folks. He told the people that they all wanted to join the church. The he asked them to tell how they got saved. Jack said he got saved while he was in the service. Terry said she had grown up in a Christian family and was saved as a little girl. Jan said, "Captain Jack said, we were going to hell if we didn't get saved and we couldn't marry his Grandsons either, so we did." The whole church started laughing. When it quieted down Karen said, "Captain Jack read to me the Roman road and we prayed together and I accepted the lord. And don't believe Jan." Everyone laughed again. The girls were told to go change, and Rev Bob asked the people to vote on excepting Jack an Terry as members. They voted yes. When the girls were ready Rev. Bob rolled up his sleeves and led Jan into the water and said, "Because of your profession of faith I baptize you in the name of the Father and of the Son and the Holy Ghost. Next it was Karen's turn. When the girls came out after changing, Rev Bob asked the people to vote on excepting the girl as members too. The vote was yes there too. When they left the church a lot of people welcomed them to the church. Jack said, "I think these calls for a celebration. Let's go out to lunch at the best restaurant in town." Terry said, "You mean the only restaurant in town."

When they got to the car, Terry said, "I brought some more towels to dry your hair and some ribbons to tie your hair into braids or ponytails if you like." During lunch Doctor Jim said, "That was the first time that I have ever seen anyone baptized. I almost went forward myself to get saved."

When they got to Jack's house, they were going to play a game, but Jim asked Karen, "What is the Roman road you were talking about?" She went and got her Bible and sat next to him and said to Jack, "I don't remember all the verses."

Jack said, "three twenty-three, six twenty-three,

five eight and nine, and ten nine and ten." She read the verses as he gave them to her, then said, "Now say this prayer with me. Dear Jesus thank you for dying for my sins. Please let me come be with you when I die. Amen." He said the prayer after her. And said, "now what?"

"Now the angels are singing." Terry said. "And you should be baptized too. Maybe in a church in Sitka. Or maybe Jack could arrange for Rev Bob to do it at the evening service tonight. If you like."

He said, "Yes, I would like that. Can you loan me some old clothes to be baptized in?

"Sure, I'll go call Rev Bob."

Jim asked, "Jan, what did Jack really say when you got saved?"

"Same as what Karen said. But the rest was true too. If you weren't a Christian, I couldn't have married you either. The Bible says not to marry unbelievers. Jack can't make you get saved, but he did say he wouldn't pay for our weddings if we didn't get saved."

"Well, now that I'm a Christian, does that mean he will pay for ours?"

"You haven't asked me yet. But if we asked him, he probably would."

Jack came back and said, "It is all set. Rev. Bob said no problem. And I called the float plane guys. They said tomorrow would be as soon as they would fly."

The Doc said, "I think I would like to stay around

for a couple of days and hang around with you guys."

"We could go fishing we haven't had much time lately. And we could take some fish to my family, and you could check on those patients there."

He looked at Jack and said, "If it's all right with you?"

"Yea, we haven't had a call. It will be a couple of days before we have to go anywhere. Have fun."

The next day Jan took the Minny and picked Jim up at the dock and they went to breakfast at the restaurant and then went fishing. No poles they used hand lines. And when they had more than fourteen fish. They headed for the village. The Doc. Asked, "Isn't there a limit on these fish?"

"Not for Indians. No not on bottom fish."

"I don't think I've ever seen this many all at once. Your family should be happy."

"We'll keep a couple for ourselves. We'll smoke them when we get home." When they tied up at the dock, they each took two fish and went to her home. He was shocked at how small it was. A one room house with six people living in it. Jan told the kids to come down to the boat and help carry the fish up. The Doc. Went to the nurse's house to check on her patients.

After they left the village Jim said, that is a small house for six people to live in."

She said, "You should have seen it with five of us girls there to. And no bathroom. It is real nice living with Jack and Terry. It makes you thankful for the small things like a shower. Our older sisters all married Jack's son and grandsons and they write us letters saying how much they like living in houses and driving cars and going to church. When you have so little grown up, it makes you thankful for what you have now. I'm glad that you saw where we grew up. Maybe you can understand us a little better."

"I'm glad I saw it to. But I loved you before I saw it and it doesn't change anything. Will you marry me? I promise that we will have a bathroom."

"Well in that case, I'll marry you, but not until Jack is well enough to run the boat with just Karen. It's not easy with just two people. You don't seem to get any sleep."

"I would like to get married in Sitka so the people who I work with can come. Is that, OK?"

"Yes, my folks and friends can fly up on the float plane. When the time comes. I think we should wait until summer. I would like my sisters to come too. And this summer Terry's daughter Mallory and her family are planning to come visit maybe we can arrange it to happen then."

"Does Jack and Terry have a big family?"

"Four kids and fourteen grandkids and spouses."

"That is a big enough family. I've got two sisters and they will want to come."

"How about your folks? Do they know that you

are talking about marrying an Indian?"

"They don't care who I marry, as long as we give them some grandkids."

As soon as they tied up at jack's dock, they took the fish up to Jack's house. Jan went around back, and Jim came out through the back door and Jan told him to grab a shovel and clear a spot in front of the smoker while she got the fish ready to smoke.

When they came in, Jack asked, "how was the fishing?"

Jim said, "man, I have never seen so many fish caught so quickly in my life. And big to."

"How were your patients?"

"They are doing good. I am going to recommend that they give that nurse a raise. She works hard and does a good job to."

"What do you think of Jan's house?"

"I think the state should build them bigger houses."

"The state doesn't help them much. They build their own houses. Maybe you and the boys could go over there and do a little room addition for them if the old man would let you." Jan was out in the kitchen. But she heard what was said. She came in and said, "I don't think he would let you. Karen was his favorite; she might be able to talk him into it." She called Karen who was in their room. When she came in, Jack asked her, "Do you think your dad would let us do a room addition on his house?"

"We could ask mom to try to talk him into it. I know she would love it especially if you add a bathroom."

After dinner they played Mexican train. Jim asked, "who did the cooking? That was the best food I ever ate." Karen pointed at Jan. Jack said,

"All of these girls are good cooks."

Jan said, "our mom made us all learn to cook. And taught us the old Indian recipes for fish. That's about all they get to eat. Maybe occasionally a deer or bear. I don't like bear."

"Do you have a good recipe for deer?" Jim asked.

"Yes, three good ones and two that I don't like. I save them for family that I don't care for."

Karen said, "we have some cousin we don't like. I'm glad that we don't live there anymore."

Jan asked, "are your two sisters married?"

"No, they're younger than me. One is out of high school and has a boyfriend. But it's hard to find a boy that's not a drunk in this state."

Karen said, "Yea, tell me about it. The big money is in fishing and logging. But in both fields, they get too much time off and spend it drinking. If you have any young male nurses at the hospital that want to become squaw men send them my way." They all laughed.

Jim took the float plane home the next day. They all liked him.

Two days later, Ketchikan called, and they packed their bags. Jan was all full of talk about marrying Jim. It was depressing to Jack. He would lose another first mate. Maybe he should sell the boat. He might talk Mallory's friend Tyler into buying it when they come up to visit this summer. The boat itself isn't worth a hell of a lot. But the business is. It's doing good.

Jan was at the wheel and Karen was going to go to bed, but being more sensitive than Jan, she could see that Jack was down in the dumps. She sat next to him on the bench in the wheelhouse and said, "I know that things don't look good to you right now. But think of the good that you have brought into all of our lives. We had nothing, and now three of us have married into your family. And Jan will be marrying a doctor. A few years ago, our futures were pretty glum. We would probably have married drunken fishermen or loggers and been stuck in the Indian Village living in a shack.

And now we are all Christians and Jim is to. So, cheer up, we thank God for you. And when the time comes for me to marry you still have grandsons left. Now I'm going to bed."

Jan had been listening, she said, "She is right you know. She is a smart girl you should sell her the boat."

Jack went below and said to wake him when she got tired.

She called down to him at three that she was tired. He had slept in his clothes, so he came right up and took over. At six Karen came up and fixed breakfast.

She asked, "are you feeling better this morning? Or are you Captain Grumpy today to?' He just growled.

The dock foreman met them at seven. He said, "We have three pallets for us down in Prince Rupert. Would you mind going to get them for us we would be as happy as a clam at high tide."

"Will there be any problem with the Canadian paperwork?"

"I'll call ahead and clear everything for you."

None of them had been to Prince Rupert before so Jack went to the office to look at their charts. The dock foreman, whose name was Jim, gave him the paperwork for the pickup. And they left for Canada.

They found their way to the right pier and when Jan showed the paperwork to a dock worker, he had the crane load the pallets right away. Since none of them had passports, they didn't try to see the town. They probably wouldn't get past the guards at the gate.

They were back in Ketchikan by noon and were soon unloaded and reloaded with a pallet for Wrangell and three for Juneau. Jack called Dan and said, "We will be there by four thirty with a pallet for you. We could eat dinner with you and Carol if you like, I'll buy."

"I'm always happy to eat with you when you're buying."

For dinner Jack had a thick steak. To build up his red blood cells you know. You have to do that when you have lost a lot of blood from getting shot. At least that was his excuse. Carol got off work and joined them. She said that she heard that a new bank was going to be built there in Wrangell. Maybe Terry could come manage it and they could move down there.

Jack said, "Our daughter, Mallory is a bank manager and is coming to visit in a couple of months. Maybe we could talk her into moving here."

Carol said, "does she have any kids?"

"Yea, three, two boys and a girl. That little girl is the cutest kid you ever saw. When her mom was three or four, she looked just like a little girl on a TV show and people would ask if it was her. So, when people would stare at, she started going up to them and asking, have you seen me on TV?" We would have to explain that she was full of shit. She still is."

Carol said, "Well I can't wait to meet her. She sounds like fun.

When they were through eating, they said goodbye and went home for the night. It was only seven thirty, so everyone took showers, and the girls did some laundry and Jack worked on his book and went to bed at nine. He set the alarm for midnight. When he went in to wake them up, he said wake up the house is on fire. They both piled out of bed in their underpants. He laughed and said, "I lied, but it's time to get up. You two might want to put on shirts though it's kind of cold outside. Don't forget your clothes in the dryer." He ran down to the boat. He wanted to warm up the motor and the cabin before the girls got there.

Jan cast off. Karen went right down to bed not even looking at jack. As Jack backed the boat away from the dock Jan came in. She said, "dirty old man. You did that just so you could look at our tits." "I'm innocent, I thought you always slept in granny night gowns."

"Liar, when we get back, I'm going to tell Terry on you."

Jack just laughed. Jan went to bed. She had to get up in four hours.

When they tied up in Juneau. It was just after eight. When they were unloaded, they were told that they had two pallets for Yakutat and three for Sitka. They could make Sitka before the docks closed so Jack decided to go there first. It meant a long run in the open sea. But if the weather wasn't too bad it was OK. As they pulled into Sitka's harbor Jan called Doctor Jim and asked if he would like to come eat on the boat or go out to dinner just the two of them. I have a new dress that I can wear. He said sure, I will meet you at the dock at six.

After dinner that night they picked Jan up at the dock and said goodnight to Jim and headed for Yakutat. It would take all night. Jack took the first watch. Karen took the second, twelve to four. Jack stayed with her for a while to make sure she was OK by herself. Jan took over at four and took them into Yakutat's dock with no problem.

Since they didn't have any freight to go back, they decided to stay a while and do the tourist thing. When they left and were on the way Jan said,

"I think that Yakutat is a cute little town. But the only thing it has got going for it is that the ferry stops there."

"What, did no handsome young men whistle at you?"

"I didn't even see any young men. Only old ones."

"There should be. There were a lot of fishing boats anchored Up the bay."

Karen said, "You should not be looking at young men anyway. You are getting married in a couple of months."

Jack said, "I can't wait to tell Jim on you for looking for young men."

Jan said, "You are not getting out of me telling Terry on you as easy as that. It is not going to work."

Karen said, "If he says anything to Jim just say he's a liar. Everybody knows that." Jack just laughed and laid down on his bunk to rest.

Jan said, "Take your boots off. You're getting mud on the blankets."

Jack said in a whiney voice, "would you take them off for me? My shoulder hurts too much to do it." She did it and growled while doing it.

They stopped for the night at Pelican and ate

dinner there so Jack could get another steak. The waitress asked, "you have been coming in here for a while. Are you hard to work for? You seem to go through a lot of help."

Jan answers, "We are all sisters and the others all got married. I too am getting married this summer. Then there will be just the two of them."

"Well, do you have any more friends who want to get a wife I'm available."

Karen said, "two of the sisters married his Grandsons. He has four more Grandsons."

"Well bring them around. How old are they?"

"Twenty-one, fifteen, thirteen, and seven. They live in Idaho."

She just grunted and walked away.

In the morning they left for Juneau. They could usually get something to hall there.

Juneau had a pallet for Skagway and three for Sitka. When they got to Sitka it was too late to unload. So, Jan called Jim and asked if he wanted to go to dinner. He said yes and Jack tied the boat to the dock for the night. He and Karen went to dinner at a different restaurant so Jan and Jim could eat alone. Jan of course had on the new dress that showed too much breast.

When Jan and Jim returned to the boat. Jack could see them coming. Walking slowly down the street holding hands and talking quietly. When they were standing on the shore above, they looked down at Jack and Jan said, "Why did you let the tide go out? Now it's a long way down to the dock." Jack said, "So I could watch you turn around and climb down the ladder. It's a nice view from here."

Jim said to Jan, "Wait, I want to go down first. You know so that just in case you fall I can ketch you." She let him go. Then tucked her skirt up under her underpants and climbed down to the dock. She then pulled her skirt back out of the tuck and walked across the dock and climbed aboard and went in without saying a word. Jack said, "She always wins you know."

Jim said, "Yea, but it is a lot of fun. I wanted to ask you a favor, would you let me come for a regular round trip with you guys? I haven't had a vacation since I went to work here, and I can't think of a more fun trip.

"Aren't you going to need a couple of days off when you get married?"

"I plan to take two weeks. And spend the whole time in bed with room service."

"When would you like to go?"

"You seem to come by about once a week. Next time you come I will be standing on the dock waiting with my bags packed."

"We will be glad to have you. Jan will call you when we get close."

Jan came out and leaned over the rail and kissed

him good night and went back in.

When they unloaded in the morning the hospital had a small pallet for the Indians again. So, they tied up at the Indian village dock by noon. They boomed the load off and Karen went up to see her folks. Her mom walked back to the boat with her. She climbed aboard and talked to Jack in private. She said, "We don't have any money, but I would love to have a room addition added to our house. Who would pay for it?"

"All these sons in laws that you are getting, all have money. They will all chip in. and come help do the work to. All you have to do is talk your husband into it."

They were home in time for the girls to make dinner.

Jack went in to work on his book. But he started thinking, He didn't need the income from the boat. He did fairly well with his writing and his wife had a good job. They had paid cash for their house. They didn't owe any money. Why was he still running the boat? Just for the adventure? What kind of adventure? He had two bullet holes in him. And three dead men to his credit. He didn't feel bad about that, the country could do better without their kind.

You aren't the judge, Jack. I need to retire. Enough thinking, he opened his laptop and started writing. At dinner he brought the subject up. He said,

"I'm thinking of selling the boat. The girls keep getting married on me. Now Jan is leaving. The boat makes enough money to support a family. So, I won't feel like I'm sticking someone with a loser. Karen can keep working on the boat and staying here and helping with the cooking and cleaning and running the backhoe clearing snow. What do you guys think?"

Terry said, "I was wondering when you would finally decide that you were old enough to retire. You are seventy-two. Isn't that old enough?"

Jan said, "They will miss you in all the ports in the Islands. You have become famous, you're Captain Jack with the big gun. Jim and I will probably never see you again."

Karen said, "The new owner of the Terry Beth might fire me. Then I would have to go back and live in my folk's one room house with an outhouse. I think I'm going to cry."

Jack says, "Now I know I'm selling the boat if I can find a big enough sucker to buy it.

The next day they got a call from Jim in Ketchikan. He said, "I have a whole load of stuff for you. Eight pallets. Get here in the morning ready to go."

Jan and Karen took the Terry Beth to the fuel dock that afternoon and filled the tanks. It was going to be a long run in the next few days. Jan was excited. Because Doctor Jim was going to be coming for a week with them.

The eight pallets were for Hydaburg, Craig, Wrangell, and Juneau.

Jim the foreman said, "ever since those articles about the shootout in Kake, came out in the paper, all the sudden everybody wants to ship with you guys."

Jan said, "was there more than one article?"

"Yea, the second one was a report from the Doctor about how badly the Captain here was shot up. Sounded bad."

Jan thought it was funny. Jack asked her, "did you write that one to?"

"I didn't write the first one. I just told the reporter what happened.

He came to the boat while you were getting your stitches out and I told him what Jim said about your wounds. And how bad they were. Look at all the new business we got because of those articles."

Jack just groaned. He said, "cast off we have a long way to go. They got to Wrangell in time to eat dinner with Dan and Carol.

Jack said, "I think you are starting to gain weight Carol. You better cut back on the food before you get fat."

"You won't believe me but it's not the food that's making me fat. It's all Dan's fault."

"I'm innocent, have you decided when you are going to sell me your boat?"

"You are my friend. I have about decided not to sell it to you. Somebody might shoot you. Carol and I and the baby don't want to lose you. Besides I don't think Carol wants you around these pretty girls all the time."

Carol said, "You're right he would get shot if he messed around."

Dan said, "What about you? Don't you get in trouble with Terry?"

"No, I'm too old. They don't want anything to do with such an old man. Maybe I had a chance with Minnow. But these two are way too young."

Jan said, "Boy you can say that again. Who would want to get mixed up with a dinosaur?"

Jack said, "Jan is getting married in June. She has a brother who will be sixteen in September, if he comes to work for me, then Maybe Karen would be safe enough from you that I could sell you the Terry Beth then."

Carol said, "don't worry Karen you'll be safe. I'll take off his peg leg and beat him with it if he tries anything."

Jan said, "you two are coming to my wedding, right? If you came to work on the boat in August for that month you would know enough to take over by September."

Jack said, "Well, I'm glad that Jan has it all planned out for you. We will make sure to stop by next week, so that you can meet Jan's Doctor Jim, He is coming with us next week just so that he can meet you."

Dan said, "That will be good. That way we can

get Jack to buy us dinner again. See you next week."

When they left Wrangell, Jack said for Karen to take first watch. He would have second and Jan the third. They were going to run all night so that they could be in Juneau in the morning and in Sitka in the evening.

They arrived in Juneau and unloaded as soon as the dock came to life.

There were four pallets for Sitka and one for Yakutat. Jan called Jim and said that they were almost to Sitka, so get ready. He was waiting on the dock by the time they were unloaded. He said that he had a pallet for the Indian village. By the time they got that loaded it was quitting time on the dock, so they stayed tied to the dock and went to dinner at a nice restaurant. Both girls dressed nice. Jack told Jim to eat a lot and take a seasick pill. Because they had two full days of open sea to navigate.

Jim slept on Jack's cot in the wheelhouse. Karen took the first watch, Jack the second. Jan the last. They arrived in Yakutat When the dock was opened for business. Jan made breakfast while the rest unloaded. They headed back for Sitka. Jan asked for the first watch so she could let Jim steer. He said, "I can see why you like this. Everything is so beautiful. Look there is a whale and it's baby going north. I think we will have to buy a boat so that we can cruise around the Islands and fish whenever I have some time off." Jan said, "The first few months you are going to want to spend all your time off in bed with me."

"Well, I'm looking forward to that.

They got back to Sitka at eight thirty at night. Jan made dinner while Karen and Jim dropped the anchor. After dinner they set up the card table and played cards and talked until after midnight. Jack decided to pull out and head for the Indian village. He took the first watch. Karen took the watch for the rest of the trip.

The village has a floating dock with a long ramp down to it, so all of the supplies for the nurse have to be carried by hand to her house. Once the pallet was on the dock, Jack and Jim and Jan started carrying the boxes up to the nurse's house. Karen went to see her folks. It was still early so no one was up. After being growled at by her dad she woke up her brothers to come help haul boxes. Jim took his medical bag up with him and checked the patients. When they left the dock, He said, "We need to pay her more. She does a good job and has no one to help her."

They arrived home by noon. Jan and Jim took showers and dressed up and took Jack's truck and went to lunch in town.

Jack went to work on his book. Karen took a shower and started cleaning house and getting dinner started. She was a good worker.

Karen told Jack to go down to the boat and bring the dirty clothes bag up. He needed his paperwork. But he complained anyway.

CHAPTER 16

That night they played Mexican train after dinner. Terry thought 'these girls have all done well at getting husbands. I really like this, Jim.'

She said, "Jim, do you own a home in Sitka?"

"No, I rent an apartment. But I am looking for a house for Jan and I to move into when we're married. When we get to Sitka maybe we will have time for me to show her what I've found."

Jan said, "you have seen what I grew up in, anything would be better than that. But I will be more than happy to go house hunting with you."

The next day Jim and the girls wandered around town shopping. They went and introduced Jim to Susan and Maggy. They all had lunch together.

In the afternoon, Ketchikan Jim called. He said, "another big load for you Jack, all over the map. They like it because you will haul freight anytime and the steamboats will only stop once a week."

"I was wondering why it was picking up so much."

"Well, the newspaper articles helped. If it slows down, you can always get shot again."

They had pallets for Wrangell, Petersburg, Juneau, Skagway, and Sitka.

The girls had filled the fuel tanks up before they left. So as soon as they were loaded, they left for Wrangell. Jack called Dan and told him that they would be there by one. They would have lunch with Carol and him. They had someone for them to meet.

Dan brought the boom truck and unloaded the pallet right onto the truck and they went to the café to have lunch with Carol. Jan said, "this is him, my future. His name is Jim Heart. He is a Doctor and I love him. I hope that you can come to our wedding. It's in June."

Dan said, "we wouldn't miss it Jan. Maybe Jim will deliver our baby while we are there."

Jim said, "will it be due then?"

Carol said, "pretty close. Maybe I'll just stay there until it comes. Can I stay with you?"

Jim said, "sure any friend of Jack's is a friend of ours. Right Honey?"

Jan said, "that would be great. And I mean it too.

They made it to Petersburg in time to unload the pallet there. They had dinner with Terry and left for Juneau at eleven at night.

Jan said that Jim and she wanted the first watch, so Jack went down and slept on her bunk. He told her to wake him at two.

She woke him at three, so he didn't bother Karen.

She got up at six and made breakfast. She and Jack had eaten when they tied up to the dock at seven thirty. Jan and Jim got up while the crane was unloading them and loading on two pallets for Sitka. Karen, since she slept the whole night, took them out through all the traffic in Juneau's harbor. Jack took his boots off and laid down on the bunk in the wheelhouse and pulled a blanket over him.

Jan said, "aren't you worried about Karen taking us through all this traffic?"

"No, you're standing right there watching. At least when you can take your eyes off of Jim."

Jim said, "I'm watching too."

"Yea, when you can take your eyes off of her."

They arrived in Sitka at four PM with Jan and Jim at the wheel. By the time they were unloaded the dock crew were headed home. So, Jack said, "Leave it tied up and let's go eat some good cooking for a change."

Jim said, "Come on, these girls are really good cooks."

Jan said, "don't pay any attention to him. He just likes to yank our chains. You know that Terry is not looking forward to him selling the boat. She will have to put up with him all the time then."

"And I will have to eat my own cooking again. She doesn't cook."

After dinner they sat in the café drinking coffee and talking until the manager came to throw them out.

Then went back to the boat. Jim picked up his bags and said goodbye. Jan walked him home. Jack told Karen, "We might as well go to bed, she will probably talk him into letting her spend the night."

She was back in less than an hour and went right to bed.

There was no freight for them in the morning. So, they borrowed a skiff and anchored out. Jim called and said the hospital would have something for them in the morning. Jack said, "Let's go eat breakfast in town and do some shopping. They were getting low on food, and they needed to do some laundry. Jack bought a small portable radio and was setting on a bench outside of the laundry mat listening to the news, when the news caster said that there was another earthquake. To watch out for a tsunami.

Jack decided to stay in port until it passed. They were back on-board putting groceries away when the first wave hit. It came sliding around the end of the Island and the groceries went everywhere. Nothing broke. Jan started to fall. Jack grabbed her and jammed her up against the wheel and held her there until it passed.

Jan said, "you can let go now. Or do you just like holding me?"

"If you look out the window you will see another wave coming. I guess I could wait until it gets here and then let go and see how far you fall."

Karen had grabbed onto the rail going down to the

fo'c's'le. When she heard that she just hung on. When that one went by, Jack said, "there will be a few more but not so big." He let Jan go and started picking up food.

After the dock workers left for the night, they tied up to the dock and went out to eat.

They ate at the café early and were back at the boat when the dock workers arrived. Jim came down to say goodbye and to give the paperwork to Jack for the Indian supplies. He said, "I had a wonderful time this last week riding with you. I wish I could take more time off and go again. Well, I'll see you the next time around." He kissed Jan and hugged Karen and shook Jack's hand and they cast off and headed south.

At the village the girl's mom came down to the boat to talk to Jack.

She said, "we have talked the old man into letting you add on to the house. As long as you pay for it."

"What changed his mind?"

"He couldn't get to the outhouse the other day because there was a bear hanging around out there. He had to pee in a bottle in front of everybody."

Jack said that he would get started on it right away. He would draw some plans, bring his little backhoe over here to dig a foundation and put in a septic system. They would need a wind generator for power to run a wash machine and lights. Jan and Karen were excited that their family would finally have a decent house. And that they would get to work with Jack and the son in laws to do the work.

Jan was at the wheel on the way home while Jack made a list of things they would need. He would have to figure up the cost and tell the boys how much they were donating. Maybe they could all come help. The girls too.

As soon as they got home Jack went right to work on the plans. He was good at drawing plans and soon had some ready to talk over with the girls.

When Jack had the plans done and the cost figured out, he called the boys. He called Eric first. He said, "the sister telegragh has already spread the word. How much is it going to cost us?"

"Forty-five hundred each. Tell the boys to come up with as much as they can, and I'll cover the rest."

Next, he called Jim and told him the news. Jim said, "when it is all done whatever the other fellows can't come up with, I'll take care of. It's too bad we couldn't have helped before."

"I know, I offered but the old man wouldn't let me do it. He had to have a run in with a bear before he would see the light."

"He didn't get hurt, did he?"

"No, just his pride. He couldn't get to the outhouse because a bear was out there. It embarrassed him having to pee in a bottle in front of the kids."

When Jim got off the phone he started laughing. A nurse stopped and said, "Is something wrong Doctor?"

"No, a bear just helped to make something right."

Getting the backhoe on and off the boat was a real trick but they made it. They also took the mixer and wheelbarrow and shovels and cement tools and went to work Jack made the septic tank out of rock and Jan and Karen mixed mud and hauled rock and so did their brothers. When that was done, they did the foundation. That took a lot of rock. Jan started hauling rock with the backhoe. With everybody helping they were done in three days. Jack got a call from Juneau. They had a big load for Sitka. So, leaving the tools they left for Juneau. They traveled all night and arrived early at the docks in Juneau. As soon as the crane operator got there, they were loaded and took off for Sitka. Jack called ahead to the lumber company there with an order for the house. All the framing materials they would need and the Metal roofing.

Eric and Minnow and the twins flew into Petersburg and were deposited at Jack and Terry's house. Eric took the speed boat and with Minnow and the twin went to the village to show the twins to Minnow's folks and all her family. When the Terry Beth arrived, everybody came down to the boat to help move the lumber up to the house. Jack got to see his new grandsons for the first time. He told Minnow's dad, "you can tell that these little guys are my grandsons because they are so cute. Just like me." He just growled something in Indian. Jan said, "for some reason he didn't agree with you. And you better leave it at that."

Jack just smiled and started hauling lumber.

By the time the lumber was all moved up to the house, Jack said that they would go home in the Minny. Jan and Karen said they would stay with the Terry Beth, and sleep there.

Terry hadn't started dinner, so they drove down to the restaurant to eat.

Terry said, "those little boys are adorable. And you look more beautiful than ever, Minnow. You are a lucky guy, Eric. Did Jack get to the village tonight?"

Minnow said, "yes, and we got all the lumber moved up to the house too. With all the help we've got I wouldn't be surprised if it doesn't have a roof by tomorrow night. I brought my bags; mom will watch the babies. With Eric and Jack supervising and all of us kids doing the work we should have no problem getting it done in one day." Jack just smiled. Eric said, "what no come back?"

"No, she will just keep talking stupid. Sometimes just ignoring her shuts her up."

Eric said, "I'll have to try that. Does it work often?"

"No, but it's always funny." Minnow didn't think so. But everybody else was smiling.

When they got home Jack and Eric took the big generator down to the Minny and loaded it on. Jack said, "the little generator on the Terry Beth won't run all of the power tools at once. We'll bring down the rest of the tools in the morning. So that they don't grow legs during the night."

The babies got them up early. So, they were loaded with tools and fed and on the way by seven. The work was already going when they arrived. A lot of hands hauled nail guns, nails, hoses, generator, compressor, cords, and levels up to the house and got everything going. The sub floor was down by noon. The walls and roof framing were up by quitting time. Jack and Eric and Minnow went home without the babies. Grandma said she raised nine kids two babies were no problem since she had three daughters and three sons to help. You couldn't count the old man.

The next day was Saturday, so Terry went with them. Not to help build but to help with the babies. At nine thirty a float plane flew in, and Jim climbed out and unloaded his bags. He said, "I just came to help with the day care. I heard that there were some twins here for me to check out." He hugged all the women shook all the men's hands, got out his stethoscope and checked the babies, and kissed Jan and got out some new tool bags and put them on backwards. Everyone was laughing. Jan told him to turn the bags around and went to see what tools he had bought.

He had a eight foot tape measure a sixteen ounce hammer, and an adjustable square. He wanted to know what was so funny. By the end of the day, they were putting on the metal roof and the siding. The windows and door were in. It was waterproof. Going home that night they took the Terry Beth so they could bring back the insulation, dry wall, hard wood flooring, and showers, sinks. Cabinets, and inside doors.

Jim and Jan and Karen slept at the clinic. And ate some of their Mama's smoked fish stew for dinner. Jim swore that it wasn't as good as Jan's.

In the morning the Terry Beth was at the lumber company when it opened. When everything on the list was loaded, Eric said, "by the looks of the rest of the house we had better get the finish lumber, paint and painting stuff and plumbing fixtures now while we're here.

With all the help they had in four days it was done. Jim turned out to be a good plumber and dry wall finisher.

The old man, whose name I can't spell, and his wife Janet inspected the Job and when Janet saw a small wood stove in the master bedroom she cried.

With all hand helping they loaded all the tools and the backhoe into the Terry Beth and headed for home. Jim and Jan brought the Minny. They had dinner that night at the restaurant to celebrate a job well done.

Jim said, "I want everyone to admit that I did a good job. Even after you all laughed at my tools."

Jack said, "you did a fine job. I hope you do as well when you pay your share of the bill."

Jim said, "Yea, I forgot about that. Thinking about how much material went into it, I can imagine it will be big."

Eric said, "knowing dad he already has the figures. How much is it?"

Jack said, "It was close to forty thousand. With the four of you son in laws, that means ten thousand each. But don't worry, I'll pay for dinner."

Jim and the women looked a little worried. Eric said, "now how much for real?"

"It was almost thirty thousand. Not counting the rental on my equipment."

Eric said, "that means with you paying a share, then it's six thousand each. You are paying a share, aren't you?"

Jim said, "I'll pay half, then maybe the Grandsons will be able to come up with their share."

Eric said, "I'll pay ten thousand and dad will pay the rest. And throw in the equipment rental." They all laughed.

Terry said, "It's about time you did something for those poor people."

Jack said, "they wouldn't let me."

Jim got a room at the hotel. The girls slept on the boat. Eric and Minnow stayed in their room with the babies whose names were Eric and Jack.

At breakfast in the morning, Jim and Eric wrote their checks to Jack and the girls looked happy. They were happy for the rest of their family. Just think indoor plumbing. They said that they would buy a washer and dryer and take them over and hook them up.

Eric and minnow and Jim took the same float

plane after breakfast. Jim said, "I feel good about the work we did. It was nice of you two to come up and help."

Eric said, "Are you kidding, I didn't have a choice, Minnow said we were coming, and you can't argue with these girls. Besides everyone wanted to see the twins. It was good of you to pay so much. Terry said that you and I almost paid the whole thing. She saw the bills. Jack got the lumber company to give him a big discount on everything. He didn't pay more than a couple of thousand. He is such a rascal."

Minnow said, "but without him it wouldn't have got done either."

Ketchikan Jim called, he said you got freight. Get your asses down here.

They put the tools back in the shed and gassed up the boat and left at midnight.

By now you know the routine. The ports and cargos varied but no one shot at them. June came around and Jan's wedding day came with it.

Everybody flew into Juneau then by float plane to Sitka. Jim had rented rooms for everybody at the hotel For Jan's family too. Jack and Terry came in their speed boat with Jan and Karen. Mickey and Sue were pregnant. Terry said, I'm not yet sixty and I'll be a great grandma. It's not fair.

At the rehearsal dinner, Mickey and Sue wanted to hear all about the room addition on the folk's house. Jim said, "Let me tell it. I did most of the finish work.

Jack and Eric and Jan did the rough work and I paid for half the cost." Jan said, "The part about him paying for half was the truth. But, Minnow and I did most of the work. Jack and Eric supervised.

Karen said, "they are both liars, me and the kids did most of the work. Jack and Eric helped a little."

Cody said, "now here's what we believe, that Jack and Eric did just about all the work while you three girls sat combing your hair and goo going over the twins and Jim painted the bathroom."

Terry said, "a whole family full of liars. You should feel right at home Jim."

The Baptist church in Sitka holds four hundred. It was full. The day of the wedding. Dan and Carol came in on the float plane that morning.

The people from the hospital and the town filled it up. Jim was a popular guy.

CHAPTER 17

The wedding dress was beautiful. Not one that you could wear out on a date after. Rev. Bob came up to do the ceremony. He would ride back with Jack and Terry and Karen. The reception was held in the American Legion Hall. It was the best they ever had. Some old folks said.

Jim said, "the honeymoon will be spent in bed at our new house. We will only get out of bed to eat, and poop. So don't come by for at least two weeks."

At the last-minute Dan and Carol showed up with two lawn chairs and wanted to hitch a ride. Dan and Rev. Bob sat in the lawn chairs in the stern and talked for the whole two-hour trip.

When they reached Petersburg Rev. Bob and Karen got out and Jack and Terry took Dan and Carol on to Wrangell. They decided to eat dinner there at Carol's café. When they started talking about the wedding, Jack said, "I think it was the greatest wedding I've ever been to."

Dan said, "it was nice, but why do you think it was so great?"

"I didn't have to pay for it."

Terry said, "just think how bad the rest of them

would have been without you paying for them. You don't need to brag about being cheap."

Jack said, "Dan wants to buy the boat. How much have you saved for a down payment?"

"Not a whole lot. Maybe Terry can give me a loan."

Jack said, "Instead of a down payment, how about twenty percent of the profit? That way you can say you are working for me, so you won't lose any business. According to the rumor, we get a lot of business because of that shoot out in Kake."

"Do you believe that?"

"I don't know, but we are getting a lot more business since then.

"Maybe I should get shot too."

"It hurts like hell; I wouldn't recommend it."

"When do you want to do it?"

"Mallory and her family are coming next week, let's wait until she leaves."

"Well, give me a call. I'll give the store my notice."

Carol said, "he is very excited about this. I sure hope he doesn't go broke the first week. We have a baby coming you know."

Mallory and Tyler and the three kids arrived the fourth of July. Karen took the boys fishing. That included Tyler. She gave them poles and showed them how to hook them up. Jack had told her that he liked Gavin the best, so make sure he caught the biggest fish. She anchored the Minny over the reef and almost right away they started catching fish. She had made smoked fish sandwiches for lunch with beer for Tyler and root beer for the boys. They were only out there for three hours. They each had three fish. They ate lunch on the way home. The fish were so big that Karen had to carry two of them up from the dock for the boys. They went around the house to the back yard and Karen showed the boys how to fix the fish for the smoker. She started the fire and got the smoker ready for all the fish. Terry and Mallory and Linn

[who was three] came out to see all the fish. Terry brought a camera and took pictures of each fisherman and his catch. Gavin did have the biggest one.

Dan called, said, "I hear that your daughter and her family are there. We would like to come meet them. Could you send Karen down for us?"

Jack said, "you need to buy your own boat. The Minny doesn't go with the Terry Beth you know."

"Since you're not asking for a down payment, I will take the money I've saved and buy one. I'm looking around."

"OK Karen is on her way."

Jack called Susan and told her that this good friend of his needed a boat like the Minny. He would bring him by later today. Make sure it's a good one. Take whatever he offers, and I'll make up the difference.

When Karen got back with Dan and Carol, she

started a big pot of smoked fish stew for dinner. After all the hellos were said, and all the oohs and ahhs over Linn were over jack told Dan that Susan had a boat for him to look at. Tyler and the boys wanted to go too. They took the truck it would haul six. Susan met them at the boat yard. She was happy to meet everyone. Especially the grandsons. She showed Dan the speed boat and he liked it at once. Tyler and the boys went looking around the yard at all the boats that were for sale while Jack and Dan and Susan went into the office to pay for the boat. Dan said that he didn't bring his money. He didn't know that Jack had a boat for him to buy. Jack told Susan to bill him. He would collect from Dan. She made out the paperwork and gave Dan the keys to the boat. Tyler and the boys were back by then. Tyler asked Susan about the fishing boats that were for sale. The boys wanted to ride with Dan in his new boat back to Jack's house. Jack grabbed two life jackets and told them to wear them in the boat. Jack stayed with Tyler while he talked with Susan.

When Jack and Tyler got home Karen said that the women were down at the dock looking at Dan new boat.

When the women got back to the house, Karen said that dinner was ready. She set up a card table and chairs for the kids and Mallory dished up bowls of stew for each one. While they ate Carol told Mallory about the Bank manager job in Wrangell.

Dan said, "Carol knows the Bank President if you make out a resume, she can make sure he gets it. And while you're here she could get you an interview. Are you interested?"

"I don't know, what is Wrangell like?"

"It's smaller than Petersburg. You can walk anywhere in town in a few minutes. Houses are cheap because there is not much business there. Most of the people who live there are fishermen. Ask Karen to bring you down there tomorrow to look the place over. It's a small bank, there are only two tellers. You would be the loan officer and Manager."

"I'll talk to mom and dad about it tonight. Dad will call you.

Jack said, "we'll come, it will be a nice outing for tomorrow.

Terry said, "I'll stay home with Linn. That is about an hour boat ride. And I've seen Wrangell." After dinner Dan and Carol went down and got in their new boat and headed for home. Everybody went down to see them off.

While on the dock Gavin said, "look Grandpa at all the crabs down there." Jack said, "yea, Karen throws all the fish gut down there to feed them. Tomorrow when we get back from Wrangell, we'll get the crab nets and catch some and have some crab for dinner. Karen makes the best sauce to go with them." Terry and Mallory worked on Mallory's resume that night so they could take it with them the next day. The next morning came, and everybody got ready for the trip. Gavin said that he wanted to stay with Grandma. So, after breakfast, Jack, Mallory, Tyler and Damian left in the Minny for Wrangell. On the way Tyler told Mallory that if she took the bank job, that Dan said he could get him a job at the hardware store if he wanted it.

Back at the house Gavin was talking Karen into taking him crab fishing.

She got two buckets and three crab traps from the shed and some fish from the fridge to use for bait. And they walked down to the dock, and she showed him what to do. He started catching crabs right away, so Karen went back to the shed for more buckets. While she was there, she got a huge iron pot and put it on the burner on the back yard bar-b-que and filled it halfway with water and turned on the burner. Terry came out and asked what's going on? Karen told her that Gavin already had some crabs, and they would cook them out here. She went down and got a full bucket to bring up. The water wasn't boiling yet so she went back down and watched Gavin. He was having a great time. He would pull up a trap and dump the crab into a bucket and reset the trap. By then another trap would have crabs. When he got one bucket so full that they were almost climbing out Karen took it to the house. When the third bucket was full, she told Gavin that when the last bucket was full to bring it and the traps up to the house. He said OK pretty girl. She said how old are you, Gavin? He said twelve. She went home. They had enough crabs to feed the whole town.

When they arrived in Wrangell, Carol met them at the dock and showed them around town. They had lunch at her café. She said, "You have an interview at the bank at one. I hope you take the job we can be neighbors and friends."

"We are already friends. I understand why Dad likes you guys so much, but I don't get why you like him. Not many do."

"He has been very generous when we needed it most. We could never repay him."

"I'm glad that you like him somebody needs to." Mallory in her early thirties was very pretty with long blond wavy hair. She had a nice figure, and she was five eight. Tall for a girl. She had two years of college and was smart. She loved her dad but was surprised when anybody else did. Her Mom and her were best of friends. After lunch Carol took her to the bank and as they walked in the President came out of his office to meet them. Carol introduced them, "Mr. Wilkins this is Mallory Philp. She is here to talk to you about the manager job." Mallory smiled at him and handed him her resume. He was not a tall man only an inch taller than her. Her low heels made them the same height. They went into his office to talk. When she left his office, they were both smiling. She went back to the restaurant and sat down with Tyler and Jack. Carol came over and sat with them. She said, "well, what did he say?"

"He said if I would sleep with him, I could have the job."

Jack said, "What did he really say?"

"I told him I would need a month to get moved. How do we get all of our crap down here?"

"Sell all the stuff you can. Have a moving company haul everything down to the pier in Seattle and we'll bring them down on the boat. You might as well sell your car and truck. There aren't any roads here. Bring your four wheelers for getting firewood. Buy a boat for getting around."

Tyler said, "I have some news too. Dan got me a job at the hardware store. We need to get our asses back home and pack." Jack had the books with him, so Dan and Carol and him went over the books while Mallory and Tyler checked out all the stores and found a real estate agent to show them some houses. One of the things they had to do was to get their house ready to sell and put it on the market. Mallory said, "It would be good if we could leave the kids here. We could get a lot more work done without them. The boys will be glad to stay with Grandpa, but I don't think he would want to take care of Linn on the boat trip down to get the furniture and back. He said it would take about a week. Maybe mom could get some more time off." The real estate lady dropped them off at the café and Mallory called Jack and checked in. Carol drove Jack to the café, and they walked down to the Minny. Carol asked, "did you find a house?"

"No, all they had were three bedrooms. We want four. Maybe you could check around for us?"

"Sure, if there is anything else we can do, just ask."

"Are you on maternity leave now?"

"Yes, why?"

"Could you watch our baby for a while? I don't want to leave her with Dad. And she will be in the way while we are moving."

"I would love to, when."

"Dad will drop her off on his way south. It will be about a week from now. I really appreciate it."

"No problem, I will enjoy having her."

"She is potty trained and will talk your head off. She takes a nap just before lunch and she minds well. She shouldn't be much trouble."

After hugs all around the Minny took off for home. Terry had called and said that Gavin had caught about a hundred crabs and Karen had them cooking for supper. Jack told Mallory and Tyler and said that Karen made the best sauce to go with the crabs and sour dough biscuits to.

Dinner was as good as Jack said. Damian said that he wished he had stayed and helped Gavin catch crabs. Jack said you can try it tomorrow.

Jack asked Gavin, "did you leave any crabs down there?"

"The bottom is covered with them." Gavin said. "There must be a million of them down there." Mallory told her mom that she got the job and that

Tyler got one too. She said, "Carol is going to look for a house for us and watch Linn until we get back. I told her that Dad would drop her off on his way down. That it would be a week or so. It will be nice living close again."

Terry said, "not as close as we were in Idaho, but only an hour away."

The kids were to stay with the Grandparents. Tyler and Mallory flew home.

Ketchikan Jim called. He said, "I have four pallets for Juneau and one for Wrangell. But that's it for this week."

"We'll see you in the morning then, thanks for calling Jim."

Gavin wanted to go. Damion didn't. they would only be gone a few days, so they didn't need a lot to take along. Jack called Dan and asked if he wanted to go along. He said yea. So, they stopped and picked him up on the way down at midnight. Karen and Gavin had taken the Terry Beth and gassed it up at the fuel dock and then came home and ate supper. More crabs. Karen brought a big pot of crab chowder to eat later.

Jack let Gavin steer for a while. Told him to watch for drift logs, other boats, whales, and see monsters and rattle snakes. Gavin was pretty sure there were no snakes out there, but maybe see monsters. Jack told Gavin that one time he was out in a storm in his fishing boat when he went by a whale going the other way. There was a friend asleep down below and when they went by the whale, he yelled down for the guy to look out the port hole. When they got into port that night he asked the fellow, "what did you see when you looked out the port hole?"

"I must have been so seeing sick that I was seeing things."

"Why what did you see?"

"I saw a huge grey wall with a big eyeball looking in at me."

I started laughing. He said, "why what was it?"

"A whale."

"A whale, He couldn't have been more than six feet away. One whack from his tail and we would have been sunk."

"I have seen them send a killer whale flying, but they don't usually whack boats.

"Is this just another of your stories Grandpa? Or is it true?"

"You sound like Karen. I never lie."

Karen yells from down below, "that's a big lie right there."

Dan took the wheel next. He had been standing back watching, so Jack didn't have to tell him what to watch for. Gavin laid down on the cot in the wheelhouse and went right to sleep. Jack went below and said to wake Karen up at three. She stayed on watch until they were almost to the dock then yelled for everybody to come tie up. Jack took the wheel and she made breakfast. Dan and Gavin tied the boat up. Jack took Dan with him to meet Jim and explain that Dan was going to be running the boat for him for a while. That he had to take some time to finish his book.

On the way up, Karen said, "if it's all right with you I would like to keep on living with you and Terry, when Dan takes over the boat. I like it there. And I can take the Minny down when he needs me. Or keep the Terry Beth up at jacks and pick up Dan on the way by. Or Dan can find someone else to work for him. I don't want to move. I do have a brother who will be sixteen in a couple of months, you will need another hand when Jack leaves anyway."

"I'm sure we can work something out Karen I will need an experienced hand. Besides, you would feel bad making an ugly old man with a wooden leg run this boat by himself.

"You are not old, just ugly."

Jack said, "Do you want the first watch, Dan?"

"Yea, I'm not sleepy. What time do you take over?"

"Wake me when we get to Wrangell. We should be there by one. We can't make Juneau before the dock closes, so we might as well hang out in Wrangell, and leave at ten PM. That way we'll be in Juneau at eight when the dock opens."

As Jack thought Juneau had a few Pallets for Sitka.

And one for Yakutat. This is good, Jack thought, it will let Dan see what some of the routine is. If they hurry, they could make Yakutat before the docks closed. They did. The sea was a little rough which slowed them a little, but they still made it. Dan had never even heard of Yakutat, so after they unloaded, they walked around town for a while and ate dinner at a small café.

Dan said, "this is a cute little town. Do you come here often?"

"About every other trip. It is a long ride in open water both up and down to Sitka and all at night. We have to be really careful of drift logs, tugboats, and whales, and pleasure craft. Between the Islands it's not as bad."

Karen said, "this time of year, it's daylight most of the time. In winter it's dark all the time, and a lot more dangerous. We spend a lot more time in some port during the darkest time of the night. Especially if it's snowing you can't see far enough ahead to stay safe." Dan was impressed. Gavin was having a blast.

Karen was at the wheel when they pulled into Sitka's harbor. Dr. Jim and Jan met them at the dock and came aboard to say hi and that they had a pallet for the Indian Village. Jack explained that Dan was taking over running the boat and that it was all Jan's fault for quitting.

Jan said, "it was not my fault. That was all Jim's fault for making me move to Sitka. I could have seen him when the boat was in town."

Jim said, "that wouldn't have lasted. She's too Horney."

Jack said, "Mallory and her husband are moving to Wrangell and as soon as we drop off this load at the Indian village, we are headed to Seattle to pick up all their junk. They have three four wheelers, three motorcycles, and a lot of furniture. I don't know if they are bringing their cars and truck."

Dan asked, "are they putting them on the boat?"

"No, I told them to sell them and fly. But they are both pretty stubborn. They may bring the truck, but they will have to take it on the ferry.

Jim asked, "when are you quitting? We will miss seeing you each week when you're gone."

"I will ride with Dan once in a while to let people that I'm still here.

Some people think that we get most of our business from that shoot out at Kake. And that if I left for good the boat would go under. Not literally but financially. So, I'm retaining a small percentage of the business and will be seen now and then."

They arrived at the Indian village in the early afternoon and Karen went to see her folks at their new house. They came down to the boat to say thanks. Janet said, "I really appreciate the washer and dryer and the indoor plumbing. Everything is great." The old man said, "now that I have the biggest house in town, they voted me chief. They even voted to give me a salary. What with the money the girls send us we are doing good? Thanks to you."

Jack said, "I'm glad that things worked out good for you. I need another of your kids to work on the boat, now that Jan is gone. This guy here is Dan he will be working on the boat until your son comes on board. This other fellow is my Grandson Gavin he is visiting for a while."

They still had time, so they went and spent the night at home. They had to pick up Linn to take to Carol on the way down. They Needed a lot of food supplies and gas too. Because it would take a few days each way, Gavin asked Dan if he could stay at his house with his sister? Dan said, he thought that Carol would be happy to have him.

They left early in the morning and dropped Gavin and Linn off with Carol who was waiting at the dock for them. Carol said, "How long will you be? You know this is the first time we have been apart for more than a few hours. Hurry back." He said, "Jack says six days. I will miss you too Honey."

This was not their first trip, so Jack decided to go straight through.

With three people to stand watch, it was four on and eight off. Jack and Karen kept an eye on Dan to make sure that he was watchful for hazards. All went without a problem. They didn't stop at the wharf. Jack got a call. The truck was waiting at the pier for them. It was like Jack thought the four wheelers, motorcycles, and furniture made a pretty full load. Mallory called, she said, "we brought the truck. We sold everything else. Will you get back before us?"

"Yes, we won't be making any stops and the ferry does."

"Did the boys come with you?"

"No, Gavin stayed with Linn. Damian stayed with Terry, he's crab fishing and fishing off the dock. Call your mom and find out how he is doing. Do you have Carol's number?"

"Yes, well we will see you in Alaska. Goodbye Dad."

Nobody wanted to stop on the way home, so they didn't. When they passed the end of Vancouver Island and hit the open sea, it was almost smooth sailing. Jack said, "the last time we came through here we had to stop and wait out a storm. At least we have Karen's good cooking. You know that if Karen quits you will have to eat your own cooking. I can't imagine that it will be as good as hers."

"She can't quit, I will give my new boat to go back and forth if I have to. I will even give her a raise. How much do you pay her anyhow?"

"Minimum wage. She's a good worker and a good cook I think you should give her twelve bucks an hour."

"Does this boat make enough for that?"

"If you can keep your wife working you should be all right."

Karen said, you've seen the books, Captain Jack makes this old tub pay. My sisters and I have been happy here. He bought our clothes, paid for the weddings, fought the robbers, and been like a father to us. I'm going below."

Jack said, "now see what you've done. You made her mad."

"I didn't you did. Since I'm captain now, I'm taking first watch."

"Wake me at eight. And don't hit anything Captain."

They stood their watches, ate Karen's good cooking and enjoyed each other's company. As the went by Ketchikan Jack called Jim the dock foreman just to check on loads. Jim said they had some coming in two days for sure.

When they arrived in Wrangell, Dan went and borrowed the boom truck to unload everything. Carol brought the kids down to the dock to watch. She

Said, "I found a nice four-bedroom house. But it's kind of spendy and it's not on the water. It does have two acres with it. Room for all this stuff."

Jack said, "let's go look at it while these two lazy people unload. Gavin, you stay and help. Karen will tell you what to do."

Carol called the owner and said she was bringing someone to look at the house. She drove Jack and Lin to the house. It was at the south end of town at the edge of the woods. It was a nice-looking house it had a two-car garage and a shop out back that was as big as a three-car garage with a driveway going around to it. Jack liked the outside. And when the owner showed then through it he liked the inside too. He called Mallory and told her about the house. He said, "it's the only four-bedroom place that's nice. There is one other but it's a dump. It's got a two-car garage and a big shop with a roll up door that you could park all of your toys in. The only thing is it's not on the water. It's up in the woods on two acres. Ask someone when you get to Wrangell."

"We get there tomorrow at noon. What do you think?"

"I think you will get here tomorrow at noon."

"About the house you Jackass."

"I'd buy it it's a nice place. Because it's not on the water the taxes will be less. And it's handy to the woods to get firewood."

"How about leaving our stuff on the boat until we get there?"

"It's already unloaded. But we can leave it at Dan's place until you decide Where to dump it. We'll put a tarp over it in case it rains."

Jack asked Dan if they could leave everything on the truck for a couple of days? He said, "We won't need the truck until you bring another load. We can ride the four wheelers and the motorcycles to my house." They got a big tarp off the boat to cover the furniture on the truck. Dan took the truck to his house too. When everything was moved to Dan's house, they all went to dinner at the café. Carol was on maternity leave, so she didn't have to serve them. Lin was a big success. She's very cute.

Gavin and Lin stayed at Dan and Carol's that night. Jack and Karen went home. They would come back tomorrow in the Minny and bring Damian and Terry. They would want to see the house and Terry would want to tell Mallory how to arrange her furniture. Jack and Terry and Carol waited at the dock in her jeep for Tyler's truck to roll off the ferry. Jack just waved for them to follow. And they drove up to the house.

The homeowner was waiting for them. After introductions let them in and showed them the house. Tyler went out and looked at the shop with Jack. Tyler asked, "how much is he asking?"

"He's asking two hundred and fifty thousand, but Carol thinks he will take two twenty-five. That's big money around here, but it's a real nice house. What do you think?"

"I like it. It will be up to Mallory She's the banker."

The homeowner came out with Mallory to show her the shop. After looking at it she came to Tyler She said, "Well what do you think?"

"I like it. How much did you get him to come down on the price?"

"He said we could have it for two hundred and twenty thousand. I think we should take it. Dad says the only other four-bedroom place is a dump."

He said, "OK, let's ask how soon we can move in."

They had enough from selling everything that they only needed a small loan of eighty thousand. Terry set it up and they were moved in three days. The kids stayed with Dan and Carol until they were moved in.

As soon as everything was in the house in a big pile, the Terry Beth had to make a run. Mallory and Tyler and the boys did the arranging. But they were in. Since Tyler was not going to work for another week, the boys and him went to get firewood. Tyler found a small trailer that he could pull behind his four-wheeler in the paper. With Damian driving the four-wheeler and Tyler his truck they got a permit from the State to cut wood on their land and went to work.

The Terry Beth picked up Dan at midnight and headed for Ketchikan.

They had cargo for Hydaburg, Klawock, Petersburg, and Juneau.

Dan hadn't been to the first two before. Jack pointed out Craig as they went by. He said, we don't get a lot of stuff for these guys, but we get some once in a while. It all adds up to making a living. And I like running around the Islands. At least it's not boring." They had to go out to sea to get around a big Island and Karen was at the wheel. She yelled, "Hey come look at this." There was a pod of killer whales attacking two grey whales. One hell of a fight. Karen turned and headed right for it Dan climbed on the roof to watch.

Karen asked Jack, "Would you take the wheel, so that I can go up there to watch too?" Jack took the wheel. He had seen a fight like that before when he had his fishing boat down in California. As they got close the killers pulled off and the two Greys turned and pulled up right beside the boat. They were winded from the fight and were breathing hard blowing spouts of water all over Dan and Karen. They came back into the cabin Karen grabbed a towel off the rack by the sink and started drying off.

Dan asked, "why did the fight break off? The killers are still following us, but way off. And the Greys look like they are glued to the boat, why?"

Jack said, "The boat makes too much noise. The killers have a leader who tells the rest when to attack. Like number two come in from the other side. Number four jump over them it messes with their minds. Number three go in from this side. The noise from the motor messes up the communications. The Greys know it, so they will follow us until it's safe."

"How do you know all of that?"

"I read it on the internet."

"You are so full of crap that your eyes are turning brown. Internet."

Karen said, "I remember him telling that story before, He got it from another boat captain. Who got it from the port Captain? He has a lot of whale stories from when he had his fishing boat."

They got to Petersburg before the docks closed. Jack took Dan to the dock foreman and introduced him and explained that Dan was going to run the boat for a while. That he needed to finish his book and get it published.

After unloading they took the boat to Jack's house so they could all take a shower. Karen first, so she could make dinner. She made Jack and Dan crack the crabs and get out the meat to make crab cakes. She had this special sauce that she put on them that Dan said, "if I wasn't already married, I would ask you to marry me just for your cooking."

Terry said, "It's a good thing that Carol didn't here you say that."

"She is a little jealous of Karen. Now that we're working together. All those sisters are pretty, not one ugly one in the family.

Jack said, "that is strange, being the old man is so ugly. It must all come from the mom."

Karen said, "Dad is not ugly. He is handsome for an Indian. He's good looking enough to get a pretty wife. He must have something going for him, they have nine kids." After dinner they went back to the boat to get some sleep. Karen set the alarm for midnight. She had the first watch. Jack got up then too. To cast off the lines. He then went back to bed. He had the next watch. Dan had the wheel when they got to Juneau. Karen was up making pancakes. Dan said, "where do we tie up?" Karen kicked Jack's cot and said, "lend a hand here mate, you have a new guy on the wheel."

Jack put on his boots and took the wheel. He said, "she is so mean to such a sweet, kind, gentle old man."

Dan said, "don't forget handsome and charming and wise."

Karen laughed and handed a plate full of pancakes and a cup of coffee to Dan.

Jack took Dan to the office to introduce him and explain that he would be taking over for a while. Back at the boat he showed Dan and Karen how to do the paperwork and where he kept the books and the money box. For buying supplies and gas. Juneau had four pallets for Sitka, and two for Angoon. Another place Dan had not been. The pallets for Angoon went on last because they were coming off first. When they left Angoon Karen called Jan and told her that they were almost to Sitka. Could she come see them? She could and did. She was at the dock when they tied up. She hugged everyone and said, "I have some news. I'm pregnant."

Karen said, "Not much of a surprise, when two healthy young people have sex, it happens. That's if they are boy and girl anyway. We have some news too. Jack's daughter Mallory and her family moved to Wrangell. We hauled their furniture and toys up from Seattle. They bought a real nice house, and both have jobs. Mallory is the manager of the new bank there and Tyler is working at the hardware store, He took Dan's old job."

"I think I'll talk Jim into flying down to meet them. Jack is always talking about how pretty his daughters are I want to see if she is as pretty as we are."

Jack said, "boy, we are not too proud, are we? Her little girl is prettier than you. Right Dan?"

"She is a doll. I think she has a chance of being Miss America someday."

Jack said, "She takes after her grandpa. That's a fact."

They decided to go eat lunch at the restaurant, so Karen stole a skiff and Jack and Jan got out on the dock and Dan and Karen anchored out and rowed in.

At lunch Karen told Jan about the whale fight. And how her and Dan got up on top of the cabin and got sprayed. Jack stayed at the wheel and stayed dry. He knew what was going to happen and was laughing at them.

Jan said, "That sounds like him, everything is a joke. Minnow tells about him holding the ladder for her to climb to the pier wearing a skirt. And she's been known not to wear underpants. Was she?"

Jack said, "I don't know, I didn't look."

"Everybody that believes that raise your hands. Yea, only Jack."

After lunch, Jan hugged everyone goodbye, and they sailed for home.

On the way Jack showed them the books and how much the trip made.

He said, "we don't ever get a full load. A few pallets here and a few there. But the cost of running the boat is low, so we do Pretty good. Good enough that we all make money. We didn't do good in the beginning. But we have built up a good business now."

As they went over the books Dan could see that he would be able to support his family just fine. Even paying Jack his twenty percent.

Jack gave a long lecture on finance. One thing he said was to set yourself a salary that you can live with and leave the rest of the money in the account for emergencies. He told Jack that he needed insurance for Carol and the baby and that they could make it on two thousand a month. Jack said, "then we'll pay you twenty-five hundred. I pay myself the same as Karen, sixteen hundred. You will need another crew member, so it will cost another sixteen hundred. That's sixty-three hundred a month. The last couple of months the boat has made over twelve thousand a month. Even with the free trip to Seattle."

"That was for free?" Dan asked.

"We haul totem poles for the Indians for free now and then. Sometimes you do things for the family. But only if you like them. If you don't like them, you charge them double."

They let Karen off in Petersburg and she brought the Minny down to pick up Jack. He went to see Mallory and the kids. Carol drove him up from the dock and Tyler drove him back. They decided to keep the boat at Wrangell. Him and Karen would go back and forth in the Minny. When her brother came to work, they would have to find a place for him to stay.

The brother's name is Mike. He will be sixteen the first of September and is looking forward to going on the boat. That means that Jack will be able to quit in just two weeks. When he could spend all his time on his book, he would finish it in a month. And get it to the publisher. It would be out in two months. He has two more that he started and would be able to get to work on them. One of them is a biography. He can't decide whether to tell the story the way he's always told them, or to tell the truth. The truth might be a little bit harder to remember. Maybe he will put off the biography until he can decide what the truth is.

They were home for three days until Ketchikan Jim called. He said, "I have six pallets for you for Juneau and one for Wrangell. See you in the morning."

On the way down to Wrangell, Jack called Dan and Mallory and asked them to bring the family and meet them at the restaurant. That he was buying dinner. Jack liked having Mallory's family here. He had missed them while being up here by himself. He missed the kids. He asked, "how are the job's working out?" Tyler said, "I see that you are bringing me some cargo tomorrow."

"Just one pallet. How is the bank treating you?" "We could use some deposits Dad how about moving some of your money down here?"

"How much do you need? I've got some in my checking account, let's see, I can write you a check for twenty thousand. Will that do for now? In a couple of months, I will get an advance on this next book. It will be another twenty. Will that help?"

"Yes, forty thousand will help. Shall I open it in your name or the boat's?"

"My name, I'm selling the boat to Dan. Make Gavin a signer but don't tell him."

"I'm sitting right here, Grandpa, don't tell me what?"

Jack said, "maybe just put a paid-on death thing on the account. Payable to Terry. I'm not sure we can trust Gavin." He handed a check to Mallory.

Dan said, "boy, I wish I could write a check for twenty thousand."

Mallory said, "come open a savings account at the bank and by the time you're as old as him you will have enough. If you only put in ten bucks a month."

Dan said, "what's the odds of me living that long?"

They left at midnight. Dan had the first watch while it was still light.

Karen had the wheel when they pulled up to the dock at Ketchikan. Dan went with Jack to Jim's office. Jack explained that Dan was taking over for a while he finished his book. Jim asked, "Do you write books? How many have you done?"

"Seven, I have one on the boat, I'll give you one."

"You can't make any money giving them away. How much are they?"

"They are ten bucks. But I'll give you one, you have been a big help getting us freight. We owe you." He sent Karen up with the book so all the boys could drool.

On the way north Jack showed Dan and Karen again the paperwork. He said, "These seven pallets bring in enough to pay our wages for the month. That's why I gave Jim the book. He gets us a lot of cargo."

They called ahead and Tyler met them at the dock with the boom truck To take off the pallet for the hardware store. Mallory and the kids came down and they ate dinner together again. Carol came too.

At dinner, Jack asked, "When are you going to have that Baby?"

"I'm going to fly up to Sitka next week and stay with Jan and Jim until it comes."

They left at ten PM. It is a ten-hour trip to Juneau. While Jack was sleeping, Dan asked Karen, "what do you think about me buying the boat? Will it make enough to support my family?"

She said, "It took in over a hundred thousand last year. How much does your family need? Running a boat as a business is dangerous work. All you have to do is run into something, like a drift log, or another boat, or a buoy, and you sink. You lose the cargo, and it would cost a lot to salvage the boat and repair it. Jack saves most of the money we make, just for an emergency. But Jack is smarter than the average bear. He never wastes money."

"Thank you, Karen." Dan said and went down to the fo'c'sle to sleep.

Juneau had three pallets for Sitka and one for Hoogah. They went Hoogah first it wasn't far from Juneau. Then went on to Sitka. Karen called Jan and said, "We will be in town in a half an hour, want to have lunch?"

"Sure, are you going to unload first?"

"Yes, make it an hour. OK?"

"OK dress nice I want to eat at the nice restaurant. A doctor's wife has to dress nice and can't be seen at a cheap café with scruffy looking people."

Karen made Jack and Dan put on clean shirts. She wore a dress.

Jan met them at the restaurant dressed very nice and driving a Cadillac SUV.

Jack said, "are you sure that you want to lower yourself enough to eat with a bunch of swabbies?"

"As long as you are paying for it, I will force myself."

"I think I will bring your dad up here to see this."

"He probably wouldn't come. I would be in trouble if he did though."

At lunch, Dan told Jan that they would bring Carol with them next week to stay in a hotel until the baby comes."

Jan said, "She would be better off staying with us. I'm sure Jim will agree."

Karen said, "It's a good thing you said that I was about to start a fight. You are getting so high and mighty and all."

Jan said, "I'm only a doctor's wife on the outside. I'm still an Indian girl on the inside. We are going to fly down to see Mallory this weekend, we could bring her back with us. Is she well enough to fly?"

"Yes," Dan said. "She would like that better than a long trip in the boat. How much does it cost?"

Jack said, "Don't worry about that. Karen will pay for it." They all laughed.

The hospital had a pallet for the village. As soon after lunch as they got it loaded, they took off. They arrived at the village at three PM. With some help from some children, they carried all the boxes up to the nurse's house and left in time to arrive in Wrangell and take the Minny to have dinner at home.

It was two days before Jim called. He said, "The steamship only runs once a week and people like that you will go whenever. We have two pallets for Craig, one for Petersburg, and four for Juneau. So, see you in the morning."

Jack called Dan and told him the news. He said they would meet him at the boat at ten PM. And so, another round started. Juneau had three pallets of booze for Skagway and four for Sitka. Getting unloaded at Skagway was tricky because of the cruise ships in the way. It made them late getting into Sitka. Karen called Jan and said they were in town but got in late and wouldn't unload until morning. Would she like to go to dinner?

She said, "Yes, Jim has the night off. We will meet you at the same restaurant in an hour. OK?"

"OK. And we will dress nice. We would not want to embarrass you. Mrs. High and mighty." At dinner Jim said, "We are flying down this weekend to see Mallory and Tyler and bring your wife back. How is she doing?"

"She is doing good. She is looking forward to staying with you. She could stay at the hotel; you don't need to put her up."

"She is better off with a doctor in the house, and we live near the hospital, so it would be closer in case of emergency."

"How much does the flight cost. Whatever it is Jack will pay for it."

Jack said, "you're right, I would. But Karen already did."

Jim said, "don't worry Karen, I already did. It's a wonder to me that Karen doesn't quit. The way you guys pick on her all the time."

Jan said, "now you know why I married you, to get away from Jack and his teasing."

"That's the only reason you married me?"

"No, I was horny too, and you were handy."

The talk got worse so we will get them unloaded in the morning and on the way home.

252

CHAPTER 18

It was four days before Ketchikan Jim called again. He said, "I been reading your book. You are a good writer. You should quit playing sailor and just write. I have a bunch of stuff for you again, so I'll see you in the morning."

The weekend had come during those four days and Jack and Terry took the Minny down to see Jim and Jan and Mallory and Tyler and the kids. They hung around to watch Carol get into the float plane with her big tummy. When the plane took off Jack and Terry hugged everybody and climbed into the Minny and went home.

In another week Karen's brother Mike would turn Sixteen and Jack can quit. He liked going on the boat, but he needed to get back to his writing. He really enjoyed writing and being seventy-two years old, it was time to take it easy. It was going to be his last trip for a while. The best laid plans of mice and men, often go awry.

The day after they returned from this trip. Dan called and said that he was coming up in his new boat. That he needed to talk to Jack about business. Jack met him at the dock, and they walked up to the house together and went into Jack's office. When they were seated Dan said, "I have decided not to buy the boat. Let me give you my list of reasons. First, Carol doesn't like me being gone all the time. Second, the hardware store wants me to be manager. Third, Running the boat is dangerous. I've had enough danger in my life. So, I quit. Here are the keys. I'm sorry Jack. I know that you wanted to retire, and this screws it up. I hope that this doesn't mess up our friendship." Jack didn't say anything. He took out the book and reached into his safe and took out some cash and counted out a stack and handed it to Dan. Then he said, "Here is half the money we took in while you were with us. Don't worry, you and Carol are my oldest friends in Alaska. I will get over it." He walked Dan down to the dock and watched him take off in his boat. When he got back to his office, Karen came in. She asked, "what did Dan want?"

"He Quit, He said that his wife was jealous of you being with him all those nights. That you are just too damn good looking to be around her husband all the time."

"You are full of shit, Jack. Did he really quiet?"

"Would I lie to you?"

"Yes, if you don't tell me the truth I'm going to quit."

"They want him back at the hardware store. They will make him manager. And Carol doesn't like him gone all the time."

She said, "now what?"

"Go get your brother. We will not go anywhere until he is old enough. That's only a couple of days."

When she left Jack called Eric. He wanted to tell someone his sad story. When he got through telling it. Eric said, well my sad story is that the company that I work for has lost its contract. I'm out of a job. How about selling me the boat? I would move up there in a minute. And you know that Minnow would love it. Jack said, "put your house up for sale. I'll start looking for a place here for you. Terry will be overjoyed to have the twins up here."

Jack called Maggy He said, "My son Eric wants to move up here, he will need a four-bedroom place here in town. Would you start looking?"

She said, "there are a few. It will depend on how much he wants to spend. It will be good to have Minnow back. There haven't been any real good fights since she left. I'll make out a list and send it to them."

Jack bought a twelve by fourteen shed from the Lumber company and had it delivered to the back Yard He wired it insulated it, dry walled it, painted it and moved his office out there and let Mike have his old office for a bedroom. Eric called, He said, we have a buyer for our house and told Maggy that we would take one that she would pick out for us. As long as it has a dock so that we can keep the boat at the house. Ask Maggy to show you the house. Make sure that it's

OK. OK?"

"Terry and I will go look tomorrow."

Jack called Terry at work. He said, "Eric and Minnow are moving in with us. Isn't that great? We will get to see the twin all the time."

She said, "What are you talking about?"

"Dan backed out on buying the boat. When I called Eric to tell him my sad story. He told me that he lost his job down there. Would I sell him the boat? Maggy has a house for us to look at for them tomorrow. We have a new roommate too."

"Start over and tell it slower, maybe then I can get it all."

In the morning they went with Maggy to look at houses. The one that Eric liked, was just fine. Terry told Maggy to start the paperwork. She told Jack to give her a check for the escrow.

Jim called so that night they headed for Ketchikan. They took the Minny down to Wrangell and picked up the Terry Beth. They would pick up the Minny on the way back. Mike had grown up around boats, so he knew what to watch out for. He took the first watch. Jack was at the wheel when they got to Ketchikan and tied up at the dock. Jim had eight pallets for them. Two for Wrangell and six for Juneau. It was almost a full load. When they arrived at Wrangell Dan met them at the dock with the boom truck and took his two pallets Karen grabbed the Minny and Jack followed her home. They went to the house for dinner and left at ten P.M.

They made it to Juneau when the dock opened. When they were unloaded and getting paperwork for Sitka, Eric climbed out of a taxi with a couple of bags. He said, "how's that for timing? I decided to fly up ahead of everybody and called Terry. She told me when you would be here, and it worked out. Terry said that Maggy had a house for us, so I came early to look things over and do paperwork, before we go down to get our furniture."

"Do you mean that you left Minnow to pack and get your furniture to the dock and everything by herself?"

"You know Minnow, When I told her that we were moving up here she started packing before I finished talking. She had everything packed before I left. She was getting the furniture loaded into crates when I left and was arranging with the dock at Bainbridge Island to load it on the Terry Beth. How soon can we get there?"

"We have three pallets to drop off in Sitka, but we can go right from there. Say four days. Call Minnow and tell her that if we don't hit a whale or a tugboat, that we will be there in four days. Tell her that Mike has joined us now. Is she coming on the ferry?"

"Yes, she is bringing my truck with all of my tools. You know that a carpenter can't go anywhere without his tools. She wanted to sell it all and ride with us. I told her she could get a cabin on the ferry and the twins would do better that way. We almost had a fight over it. But I pointed out that I'm twice her size and your son, so she didn't have a chance. She didn't like it, but she gave in."

They say that she's whipped every guy her age in town. She may try you too someday." By then they were at the boat. The cargo was loaded and tied down. Mike cast off as soon as they were on board. Jack introduced Eric to Mike and Eric hugged Karen and she asked, "So how is my sister and the twins?"

"They are doing good. You will be seeing them in about a week. How is the rest of the family? How is the new house working out?"

"Mom is loving it; you don't know how she struggled for all those years. She has a washer and dryer and electricity, and they voted my dad chief with a salary. So, they have some money now. All because you built them a house. They love you. And on top of that you took their biggest troublemaker away."

He said, "Now I'm bringing her back, with two little troublemakers along with her. She wouldn't wait with the furniture. She left on the ferry the day I left. She will be sleeping in your bed when we get back."

"I don't care. I will be glad to see her, and so will the folks. Jan and her Dr. Jim will probably fly down to see her when we get back. We'll see them when we get to Sitka. Jan is really happy that you guys are coming back. Minnow is her favorite sister."

"Are you jealous?"

"No, she is our big sister. We all love her."

Jan was at the dock when they got there. She jumped onto the boat as soon as it tied up. She hugged Eric and said, "We are all very glad that you are back. We will fly down as soon as you get back from Seattle. We are all looking forward to seeing Minnow and the twins. It's too bad that the grandsons aren't coming too. Then we would all be back together again."

"I don't think you can pry them loose from their jobs. They're doing pretty well and won't want to quit. But it would be nice." Jim came down to say hello before they left. But Eric was in a hurry to get going so they didn't talk long.

They had four people to stand watch so Jack said they would do three-hour watches. Jack and Karen did the hours after dark when it was hardest to see. Karen told Eric and Mike the story about the fight between the killer whales and the grey whales and how her and Dan got sprayed, and that Jack thought it was so funny. Eric said, "I have heard all of his whale stories before. This is at least a new one."

Karen said, "Your Dad is the Hero of our family, so talk nice or I will throw you overboard." Jack was up on the roof watching the view, so he wasn't listening. Too bad He would have thought it real funny, two hundred- and sixty-pound Eric getting thrown overboard by a one hundred ten-pound girl.

They arrived at Bainbridge Island at noon and were loaded right away. They didn't waste any time heading back north. When dinner time came around Karen had some smoked fish stew for them. Eric said, "I think that even tastes better than Minnow's."

Karen said, "don't tell Minnow that. It just tastes better at sea. We have the same recipe."

When they got to the north end of Vancouver Island the seas were running about eight foot high. Jack said, "well, It's your furniture. Do you want to hold up or go for it?" Eric said, "Tie it down better and let's go for it."

They only had thirty miles of open water before they were behind Islands again. The Terry Beth did fine. To stay out of the open sea you had to weave through a lot of Islands before you got to Petersburg. Jack was forever showing them turns to make and checking the G.P.S. To make sure that they didn't miss a turn. Jack called Maggy to ask if she could get a truck again to help. She said to pull up a few blocks south of his dock. The tide will be high, and they will have the trucks backed up to the edge of the bank and you can boom the pallets right onto the trucks. They kept a sharp look out for the trucks when they got close.

When they found the trucks, Minnow was there waiting with them. She came aboard and hugged everyone and helped boom the pallets up unto the trucks. She was driving one of the trucks, so took off with them. Eric and Mike went with her. Jack moved the boat to his dock and Karen and him rode Jack's scooter up to Eric's house. Since nobody offered to pick them up. It's all right, Jack liked riding his scooter. They could have gone in the Minny Eric's house had a nice dock. Anyway, when all the stuff was moved into the house Karen drove Jack's truck back to his house. She needed to get dinner ready. Jack stayed and helped unpack for a while until Minnow told him to go home, she would rather do it herself. They were always so close.

Eric and Minnow and the twins came to dinner. Terry wanted to see everyone. She said, "I'm glad that I talked Jack into selling you the boat. He was so reluctant."

Eric said, "Reluctant my ass, he can't wait to dump that old piece of junk on me."

Minnow said, "don't cuss in front of the babies. And it's not a piece of junk. It brought all of us girls out of a miserable life and gave us a good start. We love that old boat and your dad. When are you taking over?"

"As soon as Dad will let me. I don't even know if it makes any money."

Karen said, "this run that we just did, made enough to pay our expenses for the month. Jack showed me how to take care of the books and I am a signer on the boat's accounts. If you ask me real nice, I might tell you how much is in them." After dinner, Jack took Eric and Minnow out to his new office, and they went over the books. How the manifest on each pallet had the weight and how much they charged per pound. How the billing was done, and how much he paid the help. He said, "I pay myself the same as I pay them, so that the extra money goes into savings and is there in case of emergency. By the way I am going to buy a new motor. We have been running that one night and day for two years, it's about wore out."

Eric asked, "are you going to get a bigger one for more speed?"

"No, that one will push the boat beyond its hull speed. Bigger wouldn't help. What we need is one with a bigger generator to help run the lights and equipment. I need to talk to Susan about that. She knows all about it."

Minnow said, "Susan is my cousin. She works at the chandler shop. Jack bought the boat through her, and she supervised all the work on her. She knows a lot about boats."

Eric asked, "how much is in the savings account? Enough to buy a new motor?"

"Enough to buy a new boat."

The next day, Jack and Eric went to see Susan. She had been to all the weddings so, she knew Eric. She said that Minnow had come to see her to show off the twins. She said, "I think she's pregnant again. How big a house did you buy? You know there are nine kids in her family? She may try to outdo her mom."

Eric said, "She didn't say anything to me about it. Are you sure?"

Jack said, "congratulations, now can we do some business? We need a new motor. But we need one that has a big generator to run our equipment and lights. It also needs to be built to run night and day. What do you recommend?"

"Evinrude has a hundred and fifty horsepower one that is made for that. Do you want me to order you one?"

"Yes, do you have some literature on it? I'd like to read up on it. I've been kind of worried about that old motor lasting much longer."

Susan gave him some literature and looked up to see where that motor could be gotten from. She said, "If I order that motor now you could pick it up in Ketchikan on your next trip."

"Yea, order it."

So now this next trip would be his last. He hoped. Ketchikan Jim called that day. He said, "You guys have been gone for a week I got things piling up here. I'll see you in the morning I hope."

Jack said, "We'll be there bright and early. And thanks Jim."

Jim had eight pallets for them, one for Craig, one for Petersburg, and six for Juneau. And one for new motor in a crate for him. When they reached Petersburg, they stopped at the boat yard to have the new motor installed. It was ready by six P.M. they pulled out at midnight. They arrived at seven thirty A.M. Jack was happy with the new motor. Being new it should last a long time. Juneau had a pallet for Yakutat and three for Sitka. They stopped for the night in Pelican and ate dinner at the café there.

While they were eating Eric asked, "The waitress seems to know you, do you eat here a lot?"

"Just about every time we get some cargo for Yakutat. It's a long haul from Juneau. If we went straight through, we would get there in the middle of the night, so we stop here for dinner and some rest and then leave at midnight we get there when the dock workers get there. Then sometimes we can make Sitka before the docks close. But not often."

Karen said, "Not ever. We make it in time for a late dinner. Which we usually eat with Jim and Jan. at a nice restaurant. So, you will have to shave and put on a clean shirt. And maybe even take a bird bath too. If you forgot your deodorant, you might borrow Jack's."

"Are you saying that I stink?"

"Like the north end of a south bound skunk."

Eric looked at Jack and said, "are you going to let her talk to me like that? I'm shocked."

"I've been meaning to say something myself. The wheelhouse is kind of close quarters you know?"

They left at midnight and arrived at just after seven. They were unloaded as soon as there was someone to sign the papers. They headed for Sitka. Eric said, "I have never even heard of Yakutat before. It's a cute little town. How often do we go there?"

"Once or twice a month. Not a big money maker, but we have a reputation for doing it all. So, we go."

"The steamboats only go once a month. So, we get all the business that are in a hurry. And we do good at it.

On the way down Karen called Jan and said they would meet them for dinner, and they would make Eric take a bird bath in the sink so that he wouldn't smell so bad this time. When they met at the restaurant Carol was with them. No baby yet. Eric told them the news that Minnow was pregnant again. After all the congratulations were over, He asked Jim about getting clipped. Jim said, "yes, just stop by in the morning and we'll take care of it. I'll even give you a cut rate." Eric decided it was too late to worry about it now. He'd wait till the baby was almost here. And not tell Minnow and then try for another one.

The hospital had a pallet for the Indian village, so they would see the in laws and the new house soon. The new chief was happy to hear that minnow was pregnant again. He said he had a letter from Mickey saying that her and Sue were also pregnant. Karen and Mike thought that it was great. Lots of little nieces and nephews running around.

Jack thought it was great. Not only more grandkids, but great grandkids too. Terry would complain about being too young to be a great grandma. But would be happy too.

When they reached home, Jack and Eric and Karen

went to the office and Jack went over the books with them again. He explained again that he would remain on the payroll collecting for the freight and paying the bills. He said, "Now the only question is how much do you want to be paid Eric? Make it enough but leave some in the account for emergencies."

Eric said, "we did good selling our house down south so put a lot down here and Mallory gave us a small loan, so our expenses are low. We don't need a lot. How about two thousand a month?"

"How about three? The boat makes plenty of money so there is no reason to short yourself. Any large expenses can be paid for out of savings. Karen is a signer on the account, so you don't even need to ask me. There is cash on the boat for things like gas and food and some people pay in cash, so you won't run out. Just write it in the log so we can keep tract for taxes. You will have to pull it out once a year to scrape the barnacles off and repaint the red lead and replace the leads. It is all yours now. You can trust Karen to help remind you of everything. Don't get mad at her she will pee in your food. By the way I'm giving her a raise since she will actually be running things for a while. I made my last run. Don't run over anything and the boat will take care of you."

Ketchikan Jim called and said that he had a good load for them. Jack called Eric and said, "I'll have the kids gas up the boat and pick you up at your dock. Be there at eleven P.M. Let Karen run things until you feel comfortable with it. She is a good mate."

Eric said, "I trust her, I mean she is an old lady of about seventeen. Right?"

"Yea, and she has been working on the boat for almost two years. And she is very smart. If you piss her off, she will quit, and I will have to come back to work and that will piss me off. Good luck."

Jack stayed at his writing all day until he forgot how many days it had been. Karen came in and took out Jack's books and filled them in without saying a word. Jack stopped writing and said, "how did it go?"

Karen said, "he told me that I was running the boat. But he didn't seem happy about it."

Jack said, "I told him that you were in charge until he felt comfortable being captain. He doesn't know enough to run things yet. You're the boss until I say otherwise. Now go earn your extra pay. It's up to you to teach him and your brother the ropes. You always do a good job and I'm proud of you. There is no one else I can trust. O.K.?"

"How much of a raise do I get?"

"How much do you want?"

"I want fifteen an hour."

"All right, but you stop whining about the job. And take care of the boat. It's all we've got."

When Ketchikan Jim called a couple of days later, he said, "I didn't see you on that last trip, but it's O.K. Karen is a lot prettier than you are. If she is going to be doing the paperwork, I'm going to have to get you more work."

"I told you that I had to take some time off to finish my book. My son is running the boat, but Karen does the paperwork. Make sure nothing happens to her on that smelly old dock of yours."

"Don't worry, I already told my boys that if anything happened to her, they were fish food. How many good-looking sisters are there in that family?"

"Six, it is strange that every one of them is good looking. I've got two sisters and they don't look anything alike. In fact, I'm the best-looking kid in my family."

He called Eric and said, "Ketchikan called, Jim said that he liked Karen coming to his office for the paperwork. And he was going to have to get more freight for us so that he can see her more often. Maybe you should walk up with her once to show the boys that you're watching."

"Yea, two of them followed her back to the boat. I'll talk to Jim he seems all right."

When they got back this time, Karen came to the office wearing a new light jacket and a shoulder holster. Jack said, "what's with the gun?"

She said, we have six thousand in the strong box. I'm going to the bank and put four thousand in the savings account. We don't need that much on hand."

Jack with a big smile on his face went back to writing his book.

When Ketchikan Jim called the next time he said, "Your son came to the office with Karen last time. She said that she was showing him the ropes. I think the boys got the hint. I think he's one of the biggest guys I've seen in a while. I don't expect any trouble. Send the boat, we have a big load for you."

He called Eric and said, "Karen will pick you up at your dock at eleven again."

Eric said, "I told Minnow that Karen was being bossy. She said would you rather have me there? She is the only one who knows what to do. Does she not say please enough? I guess I will keep my mouth shut and do what I'm told without any complaints. She's right I wouldn't want her running things."

And so it went for three more weeks. Jack finished his book and sent it to his sister who did the editing. A month later he got a box of books in the mail with a letter from the publisher saying that he really liked this book it was his best yet. When Ketchikan Jim called the next time, he asked him if he knew any shop owners who might be willing to sell some of his books?"

Jim said, "Yes I know a lot of shop owners. I'll ask around.

Jack had made a wooden box with a high back with a sigh that said, Books about Alaska for sale $10. oo. So, he got everything ready and took forty books with him and dressed nice like a salesman. And went to the boat.

They picked Eric up at his dock and headed for Ketchikan. Jack was excited about selling his books. He had written many books, but these were about Alaska. The cruise ships stopped at Ketchikan and Jack wanted to sell books to the tourists. If they bought one of these maybe they would buy some of the others when they got home.

Jack took the first watch he was too excited to sleep anyway. When they tied up at the dock Jack took his box and his books up to Jim's office and gave a book to Jim. It was signed. Jim gave him a list of shops that he might try to sell books at. Karen gave him a thousand dollars for spending money. He told her he would stay for a few days and would ride the ferry home. Jim called him a cab. The first shop on Jim's list sold tourist knick knacks and when Jack asked the owner if he would sell some of his books the guy said, I will give it a try. So, Jack left him ten books and a card with his address on it to send the money to. The second place was about the same kind of place, but the owner said, "Jim called. Are you the captain Jack of the shootout at Kake?"

"Yes, did you hear about that?"

"Yea, it was in the newspapers and on the T.V. Leave some books when I tell people who wrote them, they will sell."

Jack left him ten books with a card. The next shop the owner was out. The last one was right on the edge of town and the owner said he was sorry, but he didn't sell books. He sold sandwiches and sodas and toys. He had some tables outside on the walk and there was a lady setting there waiting for her husband and her kids who were looking at toys inside. A grizzly bear came up from the river behind the shop and walked over to the woman. Her back was to the bear, and she didn't see it. It reached out and knocked her out of the chair and sniffed at her crotch and grabbed her by her leg and started dragging her toward the river. Jack stepped out of the shop just at this time He dropped his books and took out his 357 from his shoulder holster and shot the bear in the ass as it walked away dragging the lady away. The bear spun around and charged Jack. The bear stood up and grabbed Jack in a bear hug and went to bite Jack's head off, but Jack shoved his left arm up to protect his head and the bear bit down on his arm. Jack shoved the gun up under the bear's chin and blew the top of the bear's head off. The 357 hollow point can do a lot of damage. He and the bear went down sideways. The bear did a little clawing before it quit moving. Jack crawled out from its embrace and walked over and sat in a chair. The owner of the shop came out and saw the dead bear and asked what happened? The lady sat up and said, that bear attacked me and that man saved me. Two of the tourists neer by both said that they had it on video on their phones. They said they started taking pictures when the bear came out of the riverbank and filmed the whole thing. One said it was already on the internet. Someone helped the lady to a chair next to Jack. She asked, "why did the bear attack me?"

Jack asked, "Are you on your period?"

She got a little huffy but said, "yes, why?"

He said, "It's a female. They don't like the smell of a woman on her period. They've been known to kill them. It's a good thing that I forgot to leave my gun at home. Did someone call 911 my arm is busted, and my back is in ribbons. And this lady needs some attention too." He started to pass out, but the store owner grabbed him and held him up until the ambulance got there. The lady's husband came out about then and asked what happened. She said, "that bear tried to kill me. That man saved my life get out your check book and write him a big check. Ten thousand at least. He wrote the check and gave it to the ambulance driver. The shop owner took the rest of the books back into his shop to sell. He would call Jim to find out where to send the money.

When Jack woke up. He was laying on his stomach in a hospital bed. He thought about moving, but just thinking about it was enough to make it hurt. He started thinking about that bear. That first shot went right up its but. Those hollow point shells do a lot of tearing up. I'll bet it gave her a real belly ache. She might have died sooner or later just from that shot. But it wouldn't have saved the woman. When a nurse came in he asked if he could have his phone. She brought it to him, and he called the boat. He said, "I got into a fight with a grizzly and ended up in the hospital." There was a lot of yelling in the background. He said, "I got scratched up a little and a broken arm but I'm not going to die. Go on about your business and come see if I'm still here when you come by again. Bring me a hamburger the food is lousy. Call Jim at Sitka and ask him to come check on me, at least I know him. I'll call Terry. I'm sure glad that I had my 357 with me, good old Dan Wesson."

He called Terry, He said, "a female grizzly fell in love with me and when I wouldn't go home with her, she bit me. I have a broken arm and a few scratches. I asked Dr. Jim to come check on me I don't like the looks of my arm. Anyway, I'll be home when I get there. You could come see me if you want to. But I'm not dying. I think they gave me a bath in alcohol, I stink. If you come, bring me some clothes. The bear kind of tore up my shirts and Jacket. Make it a short-sleeved shirt. I have a big cast on my left arm. I love you too."

Dr. Jim showed up the next day he came in a float plane. Then a taxi. He took a look at the arm and then the x-ray. He said, the bone is badly broken. They are going to have to go in and put in a bar until it heals. Then take it back out. You are going to be here a while. Your back is tearing up too, but it will heal, and you will have a lot of scars back there. You have to learn to leave these bears alone. I heard you saved a lady's life. Captain Jack Hero."

Dr. Jim gave the family the report. He told them that Jack was going to be in the Hospital for a time. So, if they wanted to go see him he was not leaving for a while. But give him a few days for his back to heal so that he doesn't have to lay on his belly to talk to you. The first visitor was Ketchikan Jim. He said, "You don't look so good, with the wires and hoses and bandages. How do you feel?"

"About how I look. The bones in my arm are smashed. They have to do some surgeries to fix it. They said it would be easier to just take it off. If all of the surgeries don't work, they still will. I would miss that little finger, It's the one that I pick my nose with. What happened to the bear? She was a pretty color."

The shop owner sent her to a taxidermy, to be made into a rug for you. He said, He got so much advertisement from your little show, that he won't even charge you for it."

"What advertisement?"

"There were two guys doing videos of the bear when she attacked the woman. So, when you attacked the bear it all got on the video, and on T.V. You saved that woman's life. And it all got recorded. The T.V. is saying that you should get a metal. The woman's husband said he used to be against people carrying guns but he's not anymore. He said that if you hadn't shot that bear, His wife would be dead right now."

"Yea, and I might lose my arm for my trouble. But what the hell, I can still write books with one hand."

"The shop owner said to send more books he sold them all in two days after the story got on T.V. He sent some money to pay for the books. I have it here."

"Give it to Karen and tell her bring more books when you call her. If you would get them to the store owner for me, I would appreciate it."

"I will take Karen up there and introduce them. The other stores are selling them too. You better order some more."

"Thank you, Jim, you have become a good friend. And thank you for helping Karen."

"Are you kidding, if I was twenty years younger, I would divorce my wife and ask her to marry me. She is a cutey."

"Yea, and my first mate. She takes care of the books and pays the bills. She's very smart."

"Well, you look like you need rest. I'll leave you alone. I'll come by in a few days to check on you."

"Thanks for stopping by. See you later."

Jack called his wife and said, "they say if the bone graft doesn't work that they will take off my arm. That's what I get for playing the hero. But because of this, my books are selling good. If you come to visit, bring some with you. You better call the publisher and order another hundred. It looks like I am going to be here a while. You could come and give me a kiss I'm kind of lonely here."

She said, I will come on the ferry, the plane is too expensive. How do I pay for the books?"

"Take it out of my personal accounts. Karen will be putting money back in there from the book sales."

"I saw you on T.V. It was a good thing that you were carrying a gun. Because if you, weren't you would have attacked that bear with your knife, and you would have got chewed up worse. That woman's husband was on the news saying that when the cruise ship comes back to Ketchikan, they are going to come see you and thank you again. They had a fish and game guy on the news show. He said that the bear you killed had killed two other women. That the fish and game people had been hunting it and you took care of it for them. He said that female grizzlies don't like women that are on their periods. This is not the first one to kill women."

"Yea, I'm a great one-armed hero. Well, I won't die anyway. See you when you get here. I love you."

A few days later they did the work on the arm. Terry was there sitting in a chair when he came out of it. A doctor was there with her. He said, "How are you feeling?"

"Groggy, how did it go?"

"It went very well. So, you will not lose your arm. There was a lot of damage to the muscles and tendons that had to be repaired too. We worked on you for four hours. There will be a lot of recovery time. There is also some infection in your back scratches that needs to heel. I hope you didn't plan on leaving us soon."

"Right now, I don't even feel like I could walk to the bathroom."

"Well, you won't need to for a while. You have a little bag to take care of that. And you probably won't poop for a while either." The doctor left and Terry said, "well, you can quit worrying about losing your arm. I ordered more books. Karen said to leave the ones that I brought with Jim at the dock. He seemed like a nice man. He gave me some money for the ones sold. Shall I Put it in your account along with the check from the woman's husband for ten thousand dollars?"

"I didn't even know about that. When did that happen?"

"He gave it to the ambulance driver. Who gave it to the nurse? Who gave it to me? What do you want me to do with it?"

"Give it to Mallory and tell her to put it in my savings there. I don't need it. Do you?"

"No, with my salary and what Karen gives me from yours I don't need any. I am even putting money in savings. Because of your little dance with the bear being on T.V. the Publisher is even selling a lot of books and sending checks. What shall I do with them?"

"Find out if any of the kids need any help. I've got plenty of money. No one in the family should be in need. Ask Karen, the girls tell each other everything. She will know." Terry had to get back to work and left on the ferry the next day. Two days later a Mr. and Mrs. Carson came to visit. Jack was laying on his back with his arm on one of those racks that stick straight out. It hurt his back to lay on it like that, but he couldn't stand laying on his belly anymore. Mrs. Carson was the woman that he had saved.

She asked, "they said on T.V. that you might lose

your arm. How did that work out?"

"It's all here, they say that they are pretty sure that it will be O.K. Thanks for the money. The hotel bill here is liable to be kind of high."

Her husband said, "I was worried about that. Do you know how much?"

"I have insurance. It will cover it. How is your leg doing?"

"It got a little infection. But the Doctor on the boat says it's doing fine now. Thank you again for saving me. I saw on T.V. that the bear had killed other women and would have killed me too. I'm sorry that you got tore up trying to save me. We have brought you another check. I don't think the other one was enough."

"Thank you, but I'm a writer and that little show on T.V. made my book sales go through the roof. I'm doing fine. And I got a bear rug out of it."

"We want you to have the money anyway. It may help you feel better about being all tore up." She handed him an envelope, and they left. The next day Karen and Eric showed up. Eric said, "On T.V. they were talking about you having a shootout with some robbers and now getting tore up by a bear. That old Dan Wesson has saved your life more than once. How did the operation go?"

"they say that they can save the arm. But that I'm going to be here a while." He handed Karen the envelope that Mrs. Carson left. He hadn't even looked at the check. She opened it and looked at it twice then showed it to Eric.

He said, "Did you look at this check?"

"No, I told them that I didn't need any money. But they insisted."

Eric said, "what do you want us to do with it?"

He looked at Karen and said, "put it in my savings account. How much is it?"

She said, "It's only for a hundred thousand. You should go look for another rich woman to save. Nine more and you will be a million air."

"One more like this one and I'll be dead. Bring me some bullets for my gun I don't have any extra rounds."

Eric said, "you won't need any for a while. You are going to be here for a long time. Is there anything we can bring you?"

"Yea, cookies Karen knows the kind that I like. And some of your fish sandwiches. The food is bad here."

Two weeks later Dr. Jim came. He looked at everything and said, "well It looks good Jack. Is there anything that I can do for you?"

"Yea, tell them to pull this tube out of my weenie and give me my pants. I want to walk around and go to the cafeteria; I think they are trying to starve me here."

"I'll pass the word for you. Anything else?"

"I don't get much news here did Carol have her baby yet?"

"Yes, a nice healthy boy that they named Jack."

"I didn't know that they knew anybody named Jack. I need to send them some money for formula and diapers. Have you been going to church?"

"Every Sunday that I have off. And Wednesday night too."

"That makes me happy. I feel like you and Jan are my kids, and I would like it if all the kids and grandkids went to church. I want to see them all in heaven when they die. It makes me feel good that I helped." When he left the nurse came in and pulled out the tube in his weenie and gave him his pants and a pair of slippers. She helped him out of bed, and he took off for the cafeteria. He ate a sandwich and a piece of pie and drank a big glass of juice. Three weeks later they let him go home. He still had a cast but not the one that stuck out. The Doctor told him that he could go to the clinic in Petersburg to get the cast off when they said it was O.K. So, two weeks later they x-rayed his arm and said that it passed inspection and took off the cast.

The story goes on but I'm tired of writing about it. So

THE END